FALCON

OF

ERIC THE RED

by Catherine Cate Coblentz

Cover design by Phillip Colhouer

Cover illustration by Dan Burr | Inside illustrations by Henry C. Pitz

This unabridged version has updated grammar and spelling. This book contains some ideas that were held during the time period of the story but that are now considered offensive.

Originally published by Longmans, Green and Co., New York • Toronto

First published in 1942

Table of Contents

Dedicated to Rusty, "a streamlined bundle of feathered dynamite," with special acknowledgment to her owner, Henry R. Mack.

With acknowledgments also to all the old falconers whose books I have read and from whose experiences I have freely drawn, and to that modern falconer, Dr. Robert M. Stabler, who kindly offered to read the manuscript. Many of his suggestions have been incorporated.

For those who may question the location of Vineland, it can be said that the authorities on the old sagas can come to no agreement as to that location. It varies from Chesapeake Bay to the Gulf of Saint Lawrence.

Chapter I

In the Land of the White Falcons

There was a rush of wings sweeping upward. The falcon was sailing in the blue as serenely as the Valkyries, the maidens of the old god, Odin, must sail. Up and up she circled until at last there was only a speck in the heavens, a dark speck. The falcon was lost for a moment in the brightness of the sun.

Then something flashed silver where Jon's eyes kept gazing, and again the falcon was to be seen. She was watching, as Jon knew, with eager eyes for some quarry to cross the space between herself and the earth, or for the lure that would sweep about the boy in widening circles as, with practiced hand, Jon might swing the long walrus rope, at the end of which four bird wings were deftly tied. In the center of those wings, the falcon was always certain to find a piece of meat of which she might be particularly fond.

But this time there was neither quarry nor sight of the swinging lure to reward her, only the clear notes from Jon's hawking whistle cutting the air of the Greenland morning as a signal for her return. She was trained to obey and, quicker almost than it seemed possible, the great bird met Jon's gloved hand and clutched it for support.

In spite of her size, the bird met his hand lightly. Yet, at that moment, Jon stepped on a rolling stone so that it was necessary to reach out his free right hand to steady himself by means of the lichen-covered rock beside which he was standing.

Then, his balance restored, he looked down at the gyrfalcon turning her bright eyes toward his face, while her neck stretched upward a little as she waited for his words of praise and for the morsel of food which she knew would be given her.

Jon had flown many falcons for Old Olaf, but never one which had bound herself to his heart as this whitest of all the Greenland gyrs. This may have been partly because, young as she was when he had taken her from her aerie, she had fought the hardest, her down standing up until she looked like a round handful of carded wool. Yet he had managed to lift her without harm from the nest, high hidden on the Greenland cliff.

Then for a time she had been allowed the free range of an unroofed hawk pen, climbing up and down the side walls until her wings strengthened and she learned to fly, going wherever she chose, free as any falcon, except

that the jesses were always on her feet. But from habit
she returned to the hawk pen for food, and never had she
failed to find it waiting for her. Jon had caught her after
that, a second time, in a net in the hawk pen itself, and
hooded her. Then, day by day, he had taught her to know
his voice, his glove as her resting place and his hand as the
giver of food until she was eager for his coming.

Jon had found it easy to train her; for, like people, there
is a difference in falcons, and this one was unusually alert
and quick. In no time at all, the last trace of fear had faded
from her eyes, and the scared young hawk had become a
gentle, trustful one, had changed from a creature of the
wild to a bird at home among mankind and certain of their
friendship. The very turn of her head when Jon was near
showed both pleasure and trust.

On her part, the white falcon had bound herself to Jon's
heart, closer even than her talons could bind themselves
in mid-air to her quarry—to the eider, the mallard, the
kittiwake, or the ptarmigan.

She was his friend, closer to him in many ways, he
knew, even than Old Olaf, to whom he owed his very
life, or to Astrid, the daughter of their neighbor, whose
comings and goings were always as unexpected and as
welcome as the venturing close of the plover.

Aye, the falcon was his friend, and she was worthy of
that friendship. All qualities which she should possess, this
gyr had in full measure—the keen, full eyes, long wings
sharply pointed and crossed high over her train. Her flight
feathers were all unbroken and glossy. Her feet, as she had

grown older, had turned from dusty blue to the bright yellow of the healthy adult bird. Her talons were long and sharply pointed.

The unseen qualities which a good falcon must have were hers, too: speed and endurance, quick wit, boldness and strength, pride in herself and her abilities, and, most important of all, faith in her master.

As these thoughts poured through Jon's head, the bird's eyes remained intent upon his face, as though the gyr were trying with all her might to understand the strange silence. And all of a sudden, the boy's throat played him false, and words he had not intended to say broke from behind the guard of his lips.

"If I but had you for my own!" he cried.

Then he gave her the praise she expected, gave her, too, some morsels of meat, and turned to reach for the leash. But the leash was not where he had left it on the rock. Instead, Old Olaf was standing nearby, holding it in his hand. He had come up the path by the fjord, and that he had been by the rock for some time was evident when he spoke chidingly.

"Nay, do not wish for the impossible, lad," he said. "I, too, have yearned mightily toward certain falcons in my day and have hated, more than the tongue can tell, to turn such birds over to a stranger. But gyrs are only for the service of kings in distant places, and Greenland owes much to these birds. Their fame reaches so far that men throughout the whole world-circle speak of this land which Eric the Red discovered, not by the name Eric gave it, but as the Land of the White Falcons."

Jon nodded without giving answer in words, but he bent his head a little lower than usual. It was plain to Olaf that his hand fumbled before the swivel was fastened in the slit of the jesses on the falcon's feet and on the leash.

The boy kept his head turned away as he moved with a smooth, even gait toward the bird's block. Olaf noted approvingly the fashion in which the bird's feet gripped the boy's gloved finger and thumb, how easily and confidently the gyr held her place, and how deliberate and unhurried was her step from fist to the waiting block.

There was a satisfaction in her movements as she settled herself there—the same satisfaction, Olaf thought, that a human has in that which belongs to him and with which he has grown familiar, for this was the falcon's own block, and no other bird was ever placed upon it. The block had been fashioned from part of a small log that had drifted ashore and had been preserved with creosote. An iron spike, projecting from the bottom, made it possible for the block to be carried to any place and thrust into the ground. On the top, in the center, was an iron staple holding a ring, and to this Jon tied the leash quickly and expertly in a falconer's knot. No matter in what direction the bird moved on her perch, the ring in the staple moved about with her and kept her from entangling herself. She was often left thus, unhooded, to watch what went on about her, for like all falcons, the gyr enjoyed company.

"She is truly the whitest bird I have ever seen," praised Olaf. "In fact, though Eric has never had a falcon but I have trained it, I have yet to see this one's equal in any way.

Small wonder that she tugs at your heart. But consider, Jon. What could we do with the king's bird, we who live in a poor kot?"

"Well," answered Jon seriously, "the kot is small, but it is large enough to add the bird without crowding. She would be good company. I could make a padded perch for her, and she could sleep by me. She would be very quiet and not disturb you. That I know, for I have gone out many a time at night to the hawk shed, and of all the hawks, she rests the quietest, with her head usually twisted about and over her wing, her beak buried deep in her shoulder feathers. If she were by my sleeping bench, it would be necessary only to stroke her the last thing before I myself slept, and—"

"What then?" broke in a jovial voice, and out from behind the cliff strode Eric the Red himself.

Jon's heart warmed as it always did when the leader of the Greenland colonists was near. Nor was Jon alone in this. There was something in the very presence of this man which made eyes about him brighten and all hearts beat faster. Eric was one, it was told, who brought luck with him, and everyone knew it was good to be with a man who possessed luck.

So kind he was and considerate, so calm and understanding, so entirely self-controlled that it was difficult for Jon sometimes to credit Olaf's tales of how, in the old days, Eric the Red had been one quick to take offense, one whose temper, according to all reports, was as flaming as his hair and beard had been.

Neither was that redness of hair and beard easy for
Jon to picture now, for both were as white as—nay, not as
snow, not yet—but surely as white as the falcon's breast.
For Jon's quick eyes noted that, like the falcon's breast,
here and there in the whiteness of Eric's beard was still to
be seen a thin line of brown, a line not visible at all at a
distance but only perceived when one was quite near.

"If you had the king's bird in your kot, what then?"
asked Eric a second time, his voice breaking across the
boy's thoughts. The eyes of the old Northman watched the
lad before him as intently, almost, it would seem, as the
falcon had so recently watched him.

Jon felt the blood rushing in a flood to his cheeks, for
one does not speak one's innermost thoughts easily.

Old Olaf saw the flush and answered for him. "He is but
dreaming dreams," he said.

"So!" said Eric, with a quizzical smile on his lips. "He
and you grow more alike every day."

"Aye," answered Olaf, a little proudly.

"And are you still determined not to allow me to help in
making your own dream come true?" demanded Eric.

"Except that I shall buy my freedom, I shall not really
possess it," answered Old Olaf stubbornly. "It is like your
luck. In the old days, everything went wrong which came
your way, so much so that even your father declared that it
was not your fault but because your luck was bad. All your
life, he said, you would be unfortunate.

"But you yourself determined that his words should be
proven untrue. So, by your own efforts, you changed all
this and made bad luck into good. Out of your strength,

you swayed the fates and the nature of your life's journey, which had seemed so clearly destined in your youth.

"So with my own gold," he ended, "shall I purchase my freedom ale."

Eric argued no more. He was one who knew when he was bested.

"The lad is training the gyr well," Eric commended. "There shall be another gold mark added to your store when the bird is turned over to the next trader from Norway who shall anchor in the fjord.

"I have," he added, "been planning for a long time to send the whitest of all our falcons to King Olaf Tryggvason himself in return for his kindness to my son when Leif visited his court in Norway."

He was watching Jon closer than ever as he spoke and saw that, though the boy flinched at the words, he tried hard enough to hide it, and his lips made no protest.

"I am weary, Jon," declared Eric, "and my flask is empty. Would you cover the bottom of it with water?"

"Aye," answered Jon. He gave a glance toward the falcon, spreading her wings wide in the sun as though enjoying the warmth on her feathers.

"I will bring you some quickly from Shadow Rocks," he promised and reached for the empty flask.

"Shadow Rocks?" asked Eric of his falcon trainer, when the boy had set off at a run.

"It is a name the lad has given our kot by the fjord," answered Olaf. "He has named the piece of land on which our kot stands as though it were a goodly farm."

"It is a good name," commended Eric, "almost as good as Brattahlid. Tell me all you know about the lad, Olaf. I would hear once more what you remember."

Olaf complied, though there was little enough he could tell and naught but what Eric already knew. Olaf had found the boy many seasons before, cast upon the beach after a great storm, nearly hidden among the wreckage of a Northman's boat. Little more than a babe he was then, and fast bound with woman's gear to a boat's spar, more dead than alive when the trainer of Eric's falcons found him.

Yet the thrall declared that, when the boy opened his eyes, the first thing he had done was to smile and hold out his hands. After that greeting, Olaf would not turn him over to any woman in Greenland but had himself nursed the child back to life.

Ever since, the boy had remained, sharing the thrall's small kot, content as he grew older to aid Olaf in the training of Eric's falcons, gyrs, and peregrines and, from the first, showing ability and delight in every task connected with the birds.

These things Olaf recounted swiftly to Eric. "I think," he declared, "that he enjoys being with the falcons even more than mingling with the crowd which gathers in the hall of Brattahlid for a feasting. For the stories I tell there for you and your guests are no treat to him, as you well know, since he hears them many times from my lips while we work together."

"He is a likable lad," Eric nodded. "I would that I had found him in your stead. Though had I done so, I would have given him a name in honor of Thor, even as I gave the Thor-name to two of my sons, to Thorvald and to Thorstein."

Olaf nodded. "Aye," he said. "The names of the old gods are fine names, and yet it was your son, Leif, who asked that the priest of the new religion, whom he brought to this land, should baptize the child I had found. And the priest of the Christ gave him the name Jon. It is a short name and comes easily on the tongue."

"Well, Leif has no name of a god, and yet he has known the best luck of all my sons," agreed Eric. "He it was who discovered the New Land in the west. And in that land was my son Thorvald killed, while my son Thorstein lost his strength in seeking the place of his brother's burial so that he died, too."

His voice had grown slow and thoughtful, as the voices of the old sometimes grow when they look back upon the path they have taken through life, and upon the path those they have loved have taken.

"Aye," he said at length. "You did well to follow Leif's advice. Though I still follow the old gods, for all I know, Leif may have chosen the stronger leader when he chose the Christ.

"Tell me," he asked, "what does the lad plan when he grows older? He strikes me as one who loves the land more than the sea, and I do not picture him as one who will become either a soldier or a trader in foreign goods or even, in the end, a trainer of falcons like yourself."

"It is a good question," agreed Old Olaf. "He talks not much, but sometimes he declares there will come a day when he will have a farmstead of his own, with land measured by many cattle hides and burned about with fire so all may know and respect its boundaries.

"However," continued the thrall, turning his eyes toward the bird on the block as he spoke, "sometimes I have thought the possession of a farm is not so important to him as the knowledge that, with it, he must of necessity possess creatures of many sorts. Of these, he is overfond. He is as gentle with your bull as though it were a fellow being, and, though The Thunderer is ferocious enough with others and has a bellow which justifies his name, Jon rides him as easily as a well-broken horse.

"And, speaking of horses, there is not one in Greenland but will trot more eagerly to him, when he calls, than to its owner, and that even though the horse might hear him call for the first time.

"Meanwhile, as you know, he has a marvelous way with falcons, being patient and even-tempered always, and light of hand and foot. He trains them more quickly than I have ever been able, and they have such confidence in him that he can do things with them and take chances with their confidence that even I, who have had many years' experience, would not dare. He studies their natures as though they were written in runes on some rock for his reading. Indeed, I sometimes think he is like to those of whom the oldest people have told us, for he seems to understand not only the language of men but that of animals and birds.

"Aye, and of girls, as well, for Astrid Holmsdatter adores him. While Holm, because of his love for his small daughter, has told me often that he will gladly take Jon into his own hall if aught should happen to me."

"Holm might find that he would have to reckon first with me," said Eric the Red.

And though Olaf was startled at what the words implied, he said naught for a little while. After a time, he added simply, "Jon is a gentle lad."

Eric nodded, stroking his white beard with a slow hand. "And he will ever be a little lonely," he said, "despite all you or I can do."

Olaf looked at him questioningly.

"I mean by that," explained Eric, "that whoever understands the hearts of others, even of birds and beasts, must be quick to read their secret longings as well as their pleasures.

"Understanding," he said—and Olaf knew that now Eric must be speaking of the burden upon him of Greenland's colonists—"understanding carries responsibilities. That is something I have learned well."

Chapter II

The Coming of the Traders from Norway

All of a sudden, Eric looked to where a lone raven flew from a willow thicket. "Fly the gyr, Olaf," he said, "and let me see if she is really as good as the lad thinks."

Olaf went swiftly to the falcon and hooded her with a hood of soft leather covered with green pell on the outside and with a tuft of scarlet feathers rising from the top. With Eric beside him, Olaf moved the bird some distance away. When the raven was directly overhead, in a gesture swift and experienced, Olaf unhooded the gyr and cast her off straight into the wind.

There was a tinkle from the silver bells bound on her feet, just above the jesses, and the sound of the air rushing through her wings as she mounted, moving in circles until she was directly over her quarry, hastening desperately now toward a second copse of stunted trees.

But before the raven could take shelter, swifter almost than the eyes of the watchers could follow, the falcon threw herself forward and over, then stooped—that swift, downward descent which is half flight, half falling. She struck her quarry a single blow in mid-air and followed it to the earth, not far from where the two men were standing.

Olaf rewarded the falcon with a bit of sheep's heart from the hunting pouch, then placed the dead raven on the ground and allowed the falcon to deplume it there—a privilege not often given and which the bird had learned not to expect. She hunted, not as she would have hunted in the wild for food for herself but at the wish of Jon or occasionally of Olaf. And what she brought in was received thankfully enough and went, for the most part, directly into the cooking pot. It was not merely a whim which made a good falcon of as much worth as a man's horse or his best hunting dog. As for the gyr, she was accustomed to receive her care and her food from a human hand as a reward for her flying. She had every comfort a falcon might need and full security. There was no sign that she was not content.

"Aye," agreed Eric, "the boy chooses the bird-of-his-heart well. I have seen many falcons, but none which mounts so high nor stoops so hard."

"The credit belongs both to the bird and to Jon," answered the thrall.

Then Jon came hastening back with Eric's leather flask filled with water from the spring close by Shadow Rocks and with news spilling from his lips.

"Two boats are coming up the fjord—traders' boats! One is much larger than the other, and—" He paused for an instant and strove mightily to keep his voice steady for the words he must speak. "Both are, I think, from Norway."

Eric gulped thirstily from the flask. His blue eyes watched the boy. He did not miss the quick turn of his head toward the falcon on the ground, nor fail to note the swift, indrawn breath.

But Eric said only, "The water is good and cold." And to Olaf, "Come with me to greet the traders when they put in to the shore."

Olaf nodded and tossed the leather glove to Jon, who caught it and slipped it on his left hand. When the two men had departed, he whistled the falcon from the ground to his fist. To reward her for prompt obedience, he gave her a morsel of pigeon meat, and she ate this with pleasure, for she was not fond of raven.

The boy started to put her once more on the block. Then he remembered it was altogether likely that he might be called to help the traders with the boats' unloading, as he had been two or three times before when a single boat had come, filled with trading goods from Iceland. There would be no knowing when he could return to care for the bird, so it would be wiser, he decided, to take her to the hawk shed.

There were other falcons on the perch there, peregrines as well as gyrs, and to each of these he spoke in friendly fashion as he held the whitest gyr among them toward her own place on the long perch. As she stepped deliberately, almost, it would seem, regretfully, from his wrist, Jon balanced her for a moment with his bare hand until quite certain that her footing on the perch was secure. Then he fastened her properly in place with the leash, which was still attached by the swivel to her jesses, wound around the perch, and tied with the double falconer's knot.

He was free now to go to work, which usually would have delighted him, but he hesitated and looked about to see whether there were not some tasks for the birds left undone. He bent and tested the sand and gravel he had scattered that morning to be certain there was enough of each beneath the perch. Then he turned back once more to the whitest gyr and examined her feet with care in the dim light from the open door, spreading the toes apart and running his fingers between them, to see that their condition was perfect before he tested, with a finger and thumb, each pointed talon which served the bird so well.

He stroked her then, not with a feather as he had done when he'd first started to train her, but with the light, gentle touch of his fingers, slipping them lingeringly down her back and smoothing the feathers of her breast, removing as he did so a bit of raven fluff which had fallen there.

As he cast this aside, he gave a quick glance over his shoulder. Then, leaning forward, he buried his face in the soft feathers before him. Instantly, the gyr laid her own head against the lad's hair.

And then, as though regretting the gesture, after a moment she closed her beak over an unruly lock and tweaked at it briskly. The boy did not stir. The beak released the hair and, this time, sought out the top of an ear, closing upon it in a gentle pinch.

At that moment, a girl's clear call sounded: "Jon! Jon!"

"Aye, Astrid," answered Jon, jumping back from the perch and rubbing his ear.

"Two ships are come from Norway!" Astrid Holmsdatter said excitedly, appearing now at the entrance to the hawk shed, where Jon had just given the falcon a farewell stroke with his fingers.

"Hurry! Let us go and see them, Jon. It will be a marvelous sight!"

Jon frowned and shrugged his shoulders. "I shall see them soon enough," he answered, and only at the shadow on the girl's face did he realize he had been rude.

"It was good of you to come and tell me, Astrid," he said. "But you hurried too fast. You breathe like a winded horse."

As they came out in the sunlight, he added, "I vow, you must have come by the rocky path which is dangerous. You promised me after you fell and hurt yourself so badly that you would not use that path again."

Astrid stared at him in astonishment. "It is easy for you to know that I hurried," she said, "but how do you know I came by way of the rocks? Though I did not break my promise, truly. I forgot it until I was halfway here and over the worst of the path. But—how did you know?"

Jon smiled, in spite of himself, at her expression. He was pleased, too, at her astonishment. "That is easy enough.

There are fresh lichen stains on your kirtle that are the same color as the lichens which grow on those rocks, and you have torn it again, as you always do when you come by that path in a hurry."

"It doesn't matter in the least about the kirtle," the girl broke in. "It is old, seasons old. Katla will spin me wadmal for another, and we can gather dyestuffs for her, since you are so clever about them. Or perhaps the trader has some cloth from the far-off countries on his boat. I am tired of blue wadmal anyway. I would much prefer a red kirtle, one made of the foreign cloth.

"But why waste time talking of unimportant things? I thought you would be thrilled with the news of the traders. It is a long, long while since a ship has come here directly from Norway. And now not one, but two in a single day. Jon, tell me. What is the matter? Why are you not pleased?"

"Do you not realize that traders from Norway always want white falcons in exchange for their goods?" demanded Jon. "Aye, I know, walrus tusks and hides and furs of all sorts, too, but above all else, the white birds of which the kings in the east never have enough. And have I not trained the best and whitest falcon Greenland has ever produced?"

The girl stared at him with understanding on her face. So that was what had upset him! "There are other birds to be traded," she said. "The whitest of all the falcons will not go; I am certain. Eric will never send her away. He can't!"

"Aye, he can. He is sending her. He is giving her to the

king of Norway," Jon said and set his eyes hard on the
sparkling waters of the fjord.

"To King Olaf Tryggvason?" demanded Astrid, pausing
between each word.

Jon nodded.

"But he can't," protested the girl again. "He can't!"

"Why can't he?" demanded Jon gruffly.

"Because that falcon is yours. You took it from its nest.
You trained it. The bird is yours."

Jon shook his head. "Nay," he said, "the falcon is not
mine. I have nothing in Greenland of my own. Nothing!"

Astrid looked at him wistfully. She did not reply, though
she wanted to say, "You have me—for a friend."

But a friend is not what Jon needed just then. She
thought of her own treasure, her black hen, which laid eggs
as white as the tusks of the walrus. She might offer to give
him that. Then she realized how poor a bird the hen would
be, in Jon's opinion, compared with the falcon, a gyr which
Eric himself considered worthy to be sent to King Olaf.

Later, perhaps, when the falcon was gone, she might
bring the hen to Jon.

She knew a pang in her own heart at the thought, a pang
which she quickly stifled. If she felt that way about giving
up her black hen, how much worse Jon must be feeling
at the thought of turning over the falcon to strangers, of
sending it away where he could never even see it again!

Jon was walking off, moving a little stiffly and holding his
shoulders very straight. He was turning, not down the fjord
where, doubtless, the trading ships were by this time drawn

up on the sloping beach, but in the opposite direction, toward the very path he had scolded her for taking.

Neither was he whistling, as he almost always did when he walked by himself. And he never once looked behind him. It was easy enough for Astrid to understand that he did not want her to follow him. He needed to be alone.

She stood still and watched him out of sight. Then she sighed. The day had promised to be such a happy, exciting

one. Now, though the sun still shone as brightly as ever, all was changed.

Two ships from Norway had arrived—two of them. Astrid had never seen two ships come up the fjord at the same time; nor, for that matter, had many people in Greenland even seen such a sight, though Olaf and others among the oldest boasted of the great number of ships which had accompanied Eric forth from Iceland in the early days, when men, women, and children came with Eric the Red to colonize Greenland. There had been twenty-five ships then, and such a number surely had never set forth on a peaceful undertaking before. And seldom, according to Old Olaf, had a war fleet of a king been so great.

But today—two ships from far-off Norway!

Astrid blinked her eyes. She did not want to go and see them now. Not alone. With Jon it would all have been different. His quick eyes would have seen much she would otherwise fail to note. His hand would have pointed out this and that and given each the proper importance and meaning. He could have explained the use of everything to her. He would, had the strangers spoken teasingly to her, have been quick to shield her shyness. Why, Jon would have made the very sunlight ring the ships with brightness!

Now ...

Slowly and with great care, Astrid moved toward home, going not by the way she had come but by the lower, safer path.

Not a single tear did she add to those on her kirtle. Not once did she tear it. She forgot all about her wish for a new one in the more important wish now on her tongue's end.

"I wish," she whispered to nothing in particular, unless it were the wind, "I wish the traders had not come at all." Whispering helped a little, so she repeated the words aloud and sharply. "I wish the traders had not come at all—either of them!"

Not until she reached her father's sheep byre did her eyes brighten a little. She would go into the yard and talk to the black hen for a while. The hen always made such comforting, contented sounds under her feathers.

But Astrid was doomed to yet another disappointment. Only Katla's gray goose was to be seen, sunning herself in a puddle at one side of the yard. The black hen was nowhere in sight. She must have managed to fly out again and had wandered off, no one could tell where.

This wandering was a bad habit the hen had acquired. And, this day, Astrid had to search the longest she ever had for the lost one. She was very tired before she found the hen. Indeed, she might have given up the search entirely had she not kept the idea in mind that she must have the black hen ready to give to Jon when the traders should depart, taking with them the whitest of all the falcons for the far-off court of King Olaf Tryggvason.

Chapter III

At the Hall of Eric the Red

Astrid found the black hen at last by the sound of
her triumphant boasting over an egg she had laid in the
Greenland heather. The egg was still warm when Astrid
slipped it into her belt pouch before bending swiftly to
pick up the hen, which she tucked in the crook of her arm
to take back to the sheep byre. But she did not pause in
the yard with her burden. Instead, she carried the black
feathered one inside to the particular corner, walled off
from the sheep, where both the black hen and Katla's grey

goose spent the nights when they did not spend them in Holm's house.

When she came out from the byre, Katla was calling, standing on the door-stone and bidding her sister to hurry. They must make ready at once to go to the welcoming feast Eric was giving for the traders.

A welcome! Astrid made a secret face at the idea.

"Katla," she protested, "I would rather not go. I, at least, have no welcome for the strangers."

"Why, Astrid!" cried her older sister in astonishment. "They bring us grain, which we need for seed and for porridge. They bring us malt and ale and, I hear, even honeycomb, of which Old Olaf is so fond. There is iron on the ships, too, which our father declares is much needed, both for shoeing the horses and for making weapons."

To all this Astrid still continued a silent protest by shaking her head so that Katla lost patience.

"Astrid Holmsdatter," she cried, "what would Greenland do without trading ships? And these which come from Norway bring so much that Iceland can never spare us. But I am almost forgetting the surprise I have for you. I can, I think, soon change your mind about going to the welcoming."

Katla turned to the great carved chest which had been their mother's and turned back the oaken lid.

"Look!" she cried. She lifted from the top a whole armful of red cloth, span upon span of it. "You have not seen anything like this in our house before—wonderful foreign cloth, which our father just brought from the larger boat, from the trader called Karlsefni. It will make us both beautiful kirtles, and we shall still have much to keep in the chest against a grand occasion."

A red kirtle! Earlier in this day, Astrid had longed for a red kirtle and especially for one fashioned from the foreign cloth. But now she turned indifferently away.

"I would rather wear the kirtle I have," she said, "or another which you will weave for me from the wool of our own sheep."

Then, as Katla looked as though she were about to cry, Astrid relented and said, "Oh, very well, I will go with you to Brattahlid, since you are so set upon it. But I still say I am sorry the traders have come."

And, to Katla's astonishment, Astrid ended with a sudden storm of tears. It was necessary to wait for the sobbing to subside before Astrid bathed her face and put on her best kirtle, which, like the one she removed, was of the blue wadmal.

Hoping to please Astrid and take her thoughts from whatever was troubling her, Katla insisted that she wear the gold chain which had been their mother's. Usually Katla would not trust Astrid with it.

"Now," said Katla briskly, after slipping the chain about her sister's neck, "tell me. Do I look all right?"

Katla, Astrid admitted, brushing away a last tear, looked very well. Her kirtle, too, was blue—it had been easier to dye the last weaving a single color—but she wore a brooch with a yellow stone at the neck and a belt with a gilt clasp. Katla's hair was in braids and very neat, but Astrid's flowed

free and loose to her shoulders and was held in some order
by a braided band of the blue cloth, fitting close like a crown.

When Holm came to the door with the horses, both
of his daughters were waiting for him, fastening their
bright-colored mantles lined with fur, for the autumn
nights in Greenland were already sharp.

Holm rode the first horse, Astrid and Katla the second,
and in no time at all, they came to Brattahlid, set against
a mountain. Brattahlid was the largest of all the halls in
Greenland and was built on the fjord which bore Eric's

own name. It often served as a gathering place for those
settlers within riding distance.

Astrid glimpsed Jon in the crowd outside almost at
once, and he whispered to her, as he took the horse, that
Old Olaf had a new tale, one he had learned that very day
from the traders. He had sworn the newcomers to secrecy
so that no one else in Greenland knew what the story was
about, nor what news it might hold. Even Jon himself had
not heard it.

Jon spoke lightly, and Astrid understood that he wished

her to forget their talk of the afternoon concerning the falcon. So she answered as cheerfully as she could, "A new tale! That will make the feast exciting."

Her statement was true enough, for word did not come from the outside world to Greenland very often. One did not hear every season what was happening in other lands!

She heard Holm joking excitedly at the prospect, and she heard one of Eric's serving maids whisper to Katla that the young trader, Karlsefni, was already casting sheep's eyes toward Gudrid.

That was not strange in the least, Astrid thought. For Gudrid, the young widow of Thorstein Ericsson, was very beautiful, and all who saw her even once were charmed with her beauty and graciousness. There was not a young man in Greenland but would have been proud to turn her from widow into bride, but Gudrid paid scant heed to their advances.

Astrid lingered outside a bit, waiting for Jon. She meant to tell him of her adventures in searching for her black hen. But somehow, with so much excitement in the air, the doings of the black hen seemed to grow less and less important.

And besides, Jon did not return.

So, with Katla, Astrid went through the long passage which led into the hall. Then she gasped with pleasure. In spite of the cold outside, the hall of Brattahlid was warm and comfortable and blazing with light.

Every pine pillar in the two long rows which held the soot-colored roof beams of the hall boasted a torch. These cast strange, flickering shadows on every side, while, in the middle of the large room, a row of fires was burning briskly, each on its bed of stones, the smoke rising and finding its way out through the vents in the roof.

Shields and swords glittered above the wall benches, which served the men as seats by day and as beds by night. So great was the light in that hall that the hasps and the iron bandings of each man's chest, beneath his bench, could be easily seen.

But soon Astrid was looking only toward the raised platform where Eric's high seat stood, for hither he was leading his guests and giving them the best places.

Katla was busy helping Hild, the wife of Eric the Red, with the serving, but Astrid sat quietly on a stool at one end of a table of boards placed upon long trestles. Never, it seemed, had so much food been gathered together—roast upon roast of meat and fowl, fish of every kind which the fjords of Greenland or the sea provided, porridge made from grain—and everything seasoned from wild seeds, for Hild used her store of spice sparingly. Her pepper and cinnamon had come from beyond the Blue Land, to which Old Olaf had been. There was no knowing, Hild often declared, when she would be able to get more, since the folk in Europe could not obtain enough of it for themselves and were not inclined to let the trading ships leave their shores while any spice remained on board.

The Greenlanders and their guests—who, it turned out, were mostly Icelanders for all that they had but just come from far-off Norway—were drinking ale from great cups and drinking horns, but Astrid drank only skyr. That was a drink of soured milk that she liked very much, and her father declared she found color for her cheeks in every cupful.

Before the storytelling began, Eric signaled to Old Olaf, who rose and went to the little room at one end of the hall and opened the door. Then Astrid gasped with pleasure, for Jon stepped out from that room, dressed bravely and well, as though he were a member of Eric's household instead of from the kot of Eric's thrall.

His tunic was yellow and had borders of silver thread, and on his left shoulder, a piece of leather was inset. Here rode the falcon, unhooded, and looking with interest about her.

A murmur of pleasure rose at the sight of the falcon, and Eric nodded and smiled at the sound. Only Astrid noted how Jon's lips set themselves in a narrower line and how his eyes stared straight ahead.

Yet when Karlsefni, the young trader, whose name Astrid had already heard coupled with that of Gudrid, said that he would like to examine the bird closer, Jon moved promptly toward him, holding his head high.

"I have often heard," said Karlsefni, "that Greenland produces marvelous falcons, and I have seen some worthy birds from here. But never have I dreamed there was a falcon to be found anywhere as white as this one."

Jon knelt on one knee so that Karlsefni could stroke the bird on his shoulder, and never once did she offer to nip the strange fingers touching her feathers; and she took the morsel of meat the stranger offered her with care, as though understanding that Karlsefni wore no gloves.

But Astrid held her breath, knowing that had Jon ceased his low murmuring to her, the gyr might not have been so well-behaved.

Finally, Jon set the bird on a perch near Eric and seated himself cross-legged on the platform, to listen with the rest of them to Olaf's new tale.

Chapter IV

Of King Olaf Tryggvason of Norway

Olaf did not satisfy the curiosity of his audience too quickly. First, he told the old stories, in order that the traders might be reminded of the worthiness of their host and the bravery of the Greenlanders. While Astrid never could hear a story too many times, she was tired from the stress of the day, and the hall was so warm that her eyelids grew heavy, and her lashes swept lower and lower until they shadowed the bright color of her cheeks. Astrid Holmsdatter slept soundly in the hall of Brattahlid.

She might have missed the new story altogether had not Jon himself, when Olaf made ready to tell it, slipped to her side and whispered, "Astrid, Astrid. Take the sleep thorn from your ears. Waken! It is the new tale Olaf is speaking."

Even then it was hard to open her eyes, and when Jon left her, she closed them again, just for a moment. She was conscious of Old Olaf's voice long before she understood the actual words he was saying.

But all of a sudden, she rubbed her eyes briskly and sat quite straight on her stool, for Olaf was telling of another man with the same name as his own. He was speaking of King Olaf Tryggvason himself and of a battle which the king of Norway and his men fought against both the Danes and the Swedes.

"Einar the archer was beside the king," said the storyteller in Eric's hall, "and he aimed an arrow at the leader of the enemy. If he could but loose it straight to the heart, then King Olaf Tryggvason believed he and his men could win that battle, even though the odds against them were many.

"But before the arrow sped from the string, another arrow leaped through the air toward Einar, and the bow of the king's archer was broken in his very hands, split in twain with a great noise.

"At the sound, King Olaf cried, 'What broke so loudly in my ears?'

"Einar answered, casting aside the worthless bow, 'Norway, out of your hands, my Lord!' Deep bitterness was in his voice.

"'Nay, surely not,' answered the king sturdily as he tossed his own bow to the archer, asking him to use that instead.

"Einar seized the bow, but the string loosened in his fingers, and it was useless to speed any arrow. 'Alas,' he cried, 'Alas, even the king's bow is too weak for this task!'"

Astrid was not sleepy now. Her eyes were wide while her ears strained for every word. Sorry enough she was that she had missed the first part of the story, yet she knew Jon would remember and tell her on the morrow all that she had not heard.

She glanced at the falcon, and the white bird seemed to be listening, too, as the thrall's voice recounted how the warships and the long serpents of the Danes and the Swedes fought the ships and long serpents of King Olaf Tryggvason and his Northmen.

"Many were the reports of bravery which have come out from that battle, and the Swedes and the Danes are agreed that none that day was braver than the Northern King. His bright shield was held high and turned aside many arrows, his sword flashed in all directions at the same time, and his helmet, inlaid with gold, was seen gleaming as a light on the largest ship of all, where he stood in the midst of his men. His voice was raised as a trumpet in praise and encouragement. Over his armor he wore a red cloak, and though his own blood spilled crimson upon it, none could know how badly he was wounded because of the cloak's color.

"Aye, King Olaf and his men fought long and bravely. But the numbers against them were too many, even for such a leader and such followers to conquer. So, in the end, they were almost surrounded by a multitude of both Swedes and Danes, and King Olaf knew he could not hope for victory.

"But if he could not gain the day, neither would he yield it from his hands. As the Swedes and Danes made ready to rush the Northmen's boat and seize their king, Olaf Tryggvason drew close to the side of his long serpent and, with a cry of defiance, sprang fully armored over the ship's side and disappeared into the tossing waves. And such men as were still left him on that ship followed their leader and sprang after him, fully armored, into the sea.

"These things," declared Eric's thrall, "I have learned from the lips of the many who have come hither this day with Karlsefni Thordarsson, and in the second trading boat. I have woven all their reports swiftly into this tale for you, since I knew you would be eager to have it. It has been a long time since I have had a new story to tell in this hall.

"This also I have heard," he said, stopping the rising murmurs with his hand and smiling a little sadly. For he understood well the ways of men and realized how they hated sometimes to believe that those whom they had admired and loved could come no more to them. "This too I have heard, and from more than one pair of lips—for it is said that King Olaf cast off his coat of mail under the water and swam away, diving beneath the ships of his enemies, until he reached in safety a small boat, which a few of his friends held in readiness.

"Here he was taken safe on board and was rowed to a distant land, from which he will one day return. Since the time when the boat disappeared with him into the darkness, no word has been heard in all Norway concerning King Olaf Tryggvason."

The sentence hung in the air—"*No word has been heard ...*" until finally it seemed to drift with the smoke out the vent, and men stirred at the boards and looked at one another. The face of Eric was shadowed with grief, and all faces reflected his sadness. For it was understood from the story's ending that King Olaf Tryggvason was dead and would not return to his people from the land to which he had gone. He had been a brave man, a wise leader, and a great hero.

With deliberate fingers, Eric slipped a piece of gold from the bag at his belt and, with no words, pressed it into the hands of the storyteller.

Astrid's face, too, had reflected the grief of Eric the Red and of the men in that hall until, all of a sudden, it was as though she were loosed from the story's spell and realized the meaning of what she had heard.

When this happened, her hands flew together in a little spat, while at the same time, a single syllable of relief came from her lips.

Across the silence of the hall, the sounds seemed magnified. Katla turned and looked at her sister with disapproval, and Holm glanced up in surprise.

Astrid's fingers sped to her lips. But it was too late. The word had been uttered. Even Eric the Red was turning in his seat, with the carved posts rising above his head, to gaze questioningly at Holm's younger daughter.

"A piece of silver for your thoughts, Astrid Holmsdatter," he said.

Now Astrid knew her cheeks were redder than ever, and not her cheeks only but her forehead—her whole head seemed burning. Everyone in the hall was looking at her, waiting to hear what she would say.

Few in Greenland ever thought of denying Eric that which he asked, for he seldom required aught which could not be freely and readily given, and it was known that Eric himself was overly generous, but this night it seemed he requested the impossible, for Astrid shook her head slowly beneath his gaze, and her eyes pleaded.

"Will you whisper your thoughts to me then?" asked Eric. "Since I take it you do not desire to speak them aloud."

Aye, that she could do. Even though there were a hundred people in that hall, because of what her thoughts were, she could go straight to Eric.

She smiled a little as she rose, and she ran almost eagerly from her seat by the fire to the platform where Eric was sitting. Karlsefni made way for her to reach Eric's side, and once there, Astrid rested her arms on the arm of Eric's chair and put her lips to the ear of the Master of Brattahlid, who leaned toward her.

"Aye," said Eric after she had finished. "I guessed your thoughts before you slipped them in my ear. You are a friend worth having. And I would have you know that I was considering that very thing myself. You will remember this, Astrid," he said. "It is an ill wind that blows nobody good."

Astrid nodded. "I will remember."

"Now the silver," said Eric.

But the trader, Karlsefni, cried out, "Nay, I have it ready in your stead." And he held out to Astrid a piece of silver—

not of money, but a silver brooch for the neck of her kirtle, a brooch shaped like a birchen leaf. Astrid dimpled with delight and gave Karlsefni her best curtsy.

As she rose, she glanced upward for a moment at the white falcon. The bird gravely closed an eye, which, for some reason, sent both Eric the Red and Astrid Holmsdatter off into sudden laughter, while the last of the sadness in that hall must have slipped out through the smoke vents in the roof.

"What did you say to Eric?" Jon demanded as she passed him on her way back to her stool beside Katla.

Astrid shook her head. Her eyes danced. "That is a secret," she said, "between Eric the Red and me!"

Even Katla laughed at the satisfaction in her sister's voice.

But Olaf the thrall declared that Astrid was not any happier than he. For Karlsefni had given him in payment for his storytelling neither silver nor gold, but some bees' honey in the comb. Of all things he had ever tasted in his life, Olaf liked bees' honey the best.

Chapter V

The Wheel of the Seasons Turns Swiftly

There are some seasons when nothing seems to happen, when all days are alike, moving so slowly that even the change in the season itself is not realized. But there are other times when events crowd hard and fast, one upon another, until it seems that a few months are filled with enough experiences for a lifetime.

So it was the winter after the two trading ships came from Norway to Greenland. Karlsefni and the masters of the second ship had expected to pause but briefly before turning the prows of their boats back down the Greenland fjord and sailing to Iceland, which was their homeland, to spend the winter.

Eric the Red, however, urged that the season was late. The Greenlanders would be most happy to have both masters and crews as their guests until the spring.

Gudrid never said a word, but it was her very quietness, according to Katla, which did more to persuade Karlsefni than all the urging of Eric. At any rate, word was soon carried from farmstead to farmstead that the Icelanders would remain for the winter. And before the winter was more than half over, the bridal feast had been held for Gudrid and Karlsefni.

Now Karlsefni's bride had, in the old days when she was the wife of Thorstein Ericsson, set forth with him for Vineland in the west, hoping to find the grave there of his brother Thorvald. But the ship on which they had sailed had been storm-driven, so that it never reached Vineland but had finally managed to make Greenland's shores once again. That winter Thorstein Ericsson died from weakness and exhaustion brought on by his long struggle with the sea.

When Karlsefni heard from Gudrid's lips of the land in the west which Eric's son, Leif, had found, he wished likewise to sail to the New Land. Soon his interest was known all along the Greenland fjords.

So Jon was not surprised when the trader paused one day outside the kot at Shadow Rocks and asked Olaf to tell him all he knew of that land, since Olaf had a way of weaving the reports of many men together.

Karlsefni listened until Olaf had told him the tales he had heard of Vineland. Then he asked quietly, "Will you and the lad go with me to that place?"

Olaf hesitated, fighting against the longing in his heart. "Eric needs me here," he said at length. "I am his thrall, for I was taken prisoner in a fair fight on the sea in my youth, and my days were hard ones until Eric the Red bought me with a pile of gold marks."

Karlsefni smiled. "'Friend' was the word Eric used when I spoke to him concerning you," he answered. "He said to tell you that, if you felt you must have it, you might consider his permission given. Moreover, he added that he would gladly hold your freedom ale before your departure."

Olaf shook his head. "Eric may loan me to you, so be it you are minded to take me thither," he said at length. "And it may be in that land I can earn the last of the gold I yet need for buying my freedom."

Yet he shook his head again when Karlsefni offered to pay him gold in advance, as much as he needed. "Nay, I must earn my freedom fairly," the thrall repeated.

Once again, however, that season was the proffer of a freedom ale made to Olaf, and by Eric himself—Eric, suddenly brought low by an illness and doomed, it seemed, from the first, even as the sturdiest pines of Norway sometimes go down with a crash in a single storm. When he knew his illness was serious, Eric sent for Olaf and urged him to accept his freedom as a final favor.

"To take is not the same as to earn," Olaf had answered. Yet he was sore troubled at refusing what Eric termed a favor.

But Eric had held out his hand and said, "I understand how you feel, Olaf, and though I believe you are mistaken, yet knowing you, I see but honor in your answer. Sometime," he added wistfully, "you may change your mind. And if so—" But he seemed to bethink himself and set a seal upon whatever he had been about to say.

In one matter, however, Eric was firm. For, after giving Olaf the mark of gold he had promised for the training of the whitest of all gyrfalcons, he had said, "The king for

whom I destined the falcon has left this Light, so the bird is to belong to the lad Jon forever."

"The king's bird to Jon—a castaway?" Olaf asked in astonishment, thinking of the rules of falconry, which declared that only kings should fly the white bird or, for that matter, the gyrs of Iceland or of Norway, which were not so white. Princes themselves must be satisfied with peregrines.

"Aye, to Jon," said Eric. "For this I have learned. Everyone may be a king in his heart, everyone who has understanding of himself and of others."

"You were ever wise," agreed the thrall. Eric took his answer as acceptance and pressed something into his hand. He asked Olaf to call for his son, and when Leif came to his father's side, the storyteller took his departure.

What Eric told Leif then neither Olaf nor Jon were to know for a long time, but neither dreamed it could have aught to do with them. There were many matters which a dying man must attend to.

So Olaf had returned to the kot at Shadow Rocks, bringing with him the two rings of silver which Eric had given him—varvels to be fastened to the ends of the falcon's jesses. On these Jon's own name was engraved in runes. It was clear to them both that Eric had intended the gift of the falcon for some time and had ordered his smith to make the varvels and hold them in readiness.

Jon looked at the runes wonderingly. He knew that these marks would say to all who could read them that the white gyr belonged to Jon of Shadow Rocks.

But the falcon was not so gifted, and Jon whispered to her triumphantly as he put them in place. "It means that you are no king's bird now, but mine!" And having said the words once, he repeated them, adding solemnly, "Forever and forever—at least for so long as you are in this Light."

Yet when he called Astrid and she came running eagerly to his side, she did not seem in the least surprised at what Eric had done, though Jon knew she was pleased, for her eyes were like stars. But all she said was, "It must be almost as nice as having a black hen like mine."

"A black hen!" gasped Jon. "An ordinary black hen? You think—you really think your hen is as nice as my falcon?"

"Aye," answered Astrid. Her head went back in a way she had, and her voice was very firm. "The hen is *mine!* Of course it is as nice as your falcon!"

Jon closed his own lips quickly. Not the sparks now in Astrid's eyes, not the tilt of her head, but the word "mine" settled it. Naturally, she felt as she did—that which belonged to oneself was always a treasure.

"Will you come," he asked almost humbly, "and see the new leather I have from which to make jesses and a leash? After that, we will go and look at your hen. I have been thinking," he said, "that if I fix the hen a perch of her own in the yard by the sheep byre, and a nesting box by it, she may be more content to stay at home."

"I doubt if anything will cure her of straying," answered Astrid, but her words and tone were friendly once more. "Katla said that something is bound to happen to her. If she were only like Katla's gray goose. You can always find her in the barnyard puddle."

"Have you heard that Olaf and I are going to Vineland with Karlsefni?" asked Jon suddenly, though he knew that Astrid had not heard, for Eric's death had followed hard on the storyteller's decision, and folk in Greenland talked of naught else but of the loss of Eric.

Small wonder Astrid stopped still on the path and looked at Jon. "Are you speaking true words?" she demanded.

Jon nodded. "I know not how to speak otherwise."

At the answer, Astrid turned and ran blindly down the path and straight into her father, who was coming from his farmstead toward Olaf's kot.

"What is the trouble," he cried, "that you would sweep me thus from my feet?"

"There is naught wrong," she answered. "Only, Jon is going to Vineland, and—and—"

But Holm was speaking. "Well, since you two get along in Greenland, I think it likely you can manage in the New Land. I hear it is even larger than this one."

"Vineland—are you going there, too, with the Icelanders?" demanded Jon, who had come up.

Holm nodded. "Many a Greenlander is going," he answered, "for Karlsefni intends to settle in that land, even as Eric settled this one. And, in time, no doubt, the boats will ply between Vineland and Greenland, just as now they come hither from Iceland and Norway."

Aye, many events took place that winter in Greenland. After his father's death, Leif took Eric's place in the high seat and took over his duties as well. Yet he managed to be often at the fjord as the preparations for departure went on, even as Eric the Red would have been, had he still lived. The boats of the traders were newly painted and caulked, and new sails were woven for them by the women in Greenland.

Winters in Greenland were usually long, but to Astrid and Jon, this winter turned so swiftly on the wheel of the seasons that, before it seemed possible, spring was creeping along the fjords and pushing the snow up the mountainsides.

The boats of the traders were all but ready to sail. The many bundles had been taken on board, as well as the cows and sheep. For these, together with the bull, The Thunderer, Karlsefni had traded a goodly portion of the cargo he had brought from Norway.

Jon brought his falcon and set her proudly on the padded perch near the prow where, properly fastened, she could see all that went on about her, and where he and Astrid could share with the gyr the delights of the voyage.

He fastened her in place hurriedly, however, for The Thunderer was refusing to go up the gangplank. He bellowed louder, it seemed, than ever before and planted his front feet firmly on the earth.

But when Jon came running to him and put his fingers on his nose, talking quietly for a little, to the surprise of everyone except perhaps Old Olaf, The Thunderer followed the boy up the plank and took his place calmly enough among the cows.

Karlsefni made a sign to the women waiting at one side to go on board, while the men already there began taking their seats on the rowing benches.

"Is everyone aboard?" asked Karlsefni. Then Olaf began calling out from memory the names of those who were going. But before he had finished, Jon interrupted.

"Nay, we are not all here! Astrid and Katla are not on the boat. They went back for Astrid's black hen at the same time I went for my falcon. It must be the hen has strayed again, and they are hunting for her."

"A hen, did you say? Are we to miss the tide because of a hen?" demanded one of the men.

But just then the two girls came in sight. Jon drew a breath of relief, but then he made out that Astrid was carrying only a folded mantle in her arms. And as he saw Katla's arm go across Astrid's shoulder, he knew that the black hen had not been found. Yet the time had come when Astrid could search no longer and must leave behind the hen which she had boasted was to be the first hen ever to journey to the New Land which Leif Ericsson had discovered.

The gangplank itself was clear, but Holm and Karlsefni were standing at the foot of it. Jon balanced himself for a moment on the boat's edge and then jumped into the water, wading ashore to meet the two.

Without a word, he took Katla's goose and the extra mantle and followed the girls aboard. There was nothing he could say to comfort Holm's younger daughter.

"Why so sad, Astrid Holmsdatter?" Olaf asked, coming now from checking the knots of the walrus ropes fastening the cattle in place.

"My hen—" began Astrid.

She could say no more, and Jon added, "She has strayed again, and they could not find her."

"It's an ill wind," repeated somebody, "that blows nobody good. Somebody or something will have a bountiful dinner." But Jon frowned, and another, trying to mend matters, said, "At any rate, the boat is crowded, and now we shall all have a feather's breath more room."

Astrid nodded at the laughter which greeted this and tried to keep her distress to herself. Only Katla and Jon understood how she felt when the men on the shore pushed the two traders' boats through the shallow water toward the fjord's center while the rowers dipped their oars.

Then the Greenlanders who were not going to Vineland set up a cheer as the boats floated free and moved down the fjord, a cheer and a farewell, which those on board, both Greenlanders and Icelanders, the men and women, the two girls and Jon alike, echoed.

"Far Heil," came the words of those who were staying home. "Far Heil! Luck go with you. Luck!"

The priest of the White Christ made the sign of the Christian cross and raised his hand in blessing.

Jon was standing close by Astrid, but he did not look at her, though he knew her shoulders were shaking. This time it was his turn to hold back the words which had been on his lips. He understood well enough that Astrid wanted no share in his white falcon. After all, hens were rare enough in Greenland. Hild, the wife of Eric, had given Astrid's to her when it was a tiny chick, as fluffy as the falcon had been when he had taken her from the nest.

He thought then of the lamb he had carried on board. When the proper time came, he would bring this to her.

And then he saw Arn Steinsson on the shore, farther down than any of the others had been. He made a trumpet of his hands and called to Arn in his loudest voice, asking him to find Astrid's black hen and keep it safe.

Arn nodded and called through his hands back to the boat, "Aye, have no fear; I shall find her."

"Arn is good to all his creatures," declared Olaf, "and he will treasure your hen, since his small son needs white eggs for his growing."

"She lays the best eggs in all Greenland," answered Astrid.

After a time, her eyes ceased watching the shore, and she turned them instead to the prow of their boat and watched how it cut through the water.

The falcon on her perch spread wide her wings, as though she, too, would help speed their boat down the fjord and perchance overtake the one ahead. After a while, Gudrid came and stood beside the bird and began to sing.

Jon saw Karlsefni, who was at the tiller, cast a glance with pride toward the wife he had won in Greenland who was going with him to share in founding a colony in the New Land.

Jon looked at her, too, and looked at Olaf and hoped that Olaf could finally earn his freedom in Vineland. If only Astrid had not been so disappointed. Even Gudrid's singing could not wipe the troubled shadow entirely from her face.

Chapter VI

The Journey to Vineland the Good

That night when the stars came out and the falcon slept on her perch with her head buried in her feathers, Olaf began telling riddles. He watched Astrid as he did this, and, as he had hoped, she turned quickly to listen and guessed the first one while Jon was just beginning to cudgel his brain for an answer.

Olaf usually told old, old riddles. That was because the Northmen, when they had journeyed from Norway to Iceland, had remembered in the New Land the riddles they had heard in the Old. Olaf had learned them in Iceland, and in time, Iceland became the Old Country for him as he repeated what he had learned in Eric's Greenland. And occasionally when, as on this voyage, he had need of something different, he could remember riddles which, until at that moment, had seemed entirely forgotten.

Olaf almost never told the answers to his riddles but made his listeners guess and guess until they themselves found the right answer. Often it took a very long time.

"Here is a hard one," he warned.

> "What lives on the high mountains,
> And in the deep dales,
> Is without breath,
> And is never silent?"

Jon guessed wildly one answer and then another, but Olaf kept shaking his head until he declared his neck bones were creaking. Astrid said never a word, but she was thinking hard.

Finally, Jon turned to her. "Don't you know?" he asked in such a tone of bewilderment that, for the first time on the journey, Astrid laughed.

Old Olaf was so pleased that he nearly broke one of his own rules when he said, "I see I shall have to help such silly ones a little. There are four answers, because this riddle has four parts."

"Well, it is no wonder we couldn't guess!" cried Astrid. "That was not really fair. You should have told us before. I can guess the first part right away. Ravens live on the high mountains. I have seen the falcon chase them home. But I have seen more dew than anything else in the deepest dales."

"Ravens is the answer to one part, and dew is the answer, too," Olaf laughed.

"Well," declared Jon after a long silence, "fish are without breath in water, and waterfalls are never silent."

And those were the right answers.

"What has ten tongues, twenty eyes, and forty feet?" asked Olaf.

That took a long, long time to answer. Finally, Katla nudged Astrid and said, "Ask him if he saw that riddle in a pigpen?"

And the answer was, of course, that it was a mother pig with nine baby pigs.

"What are the playsters that pass over the lands playing at will? They wear white shields in winter and dark ones in summer."

Jon thought at once of the ptarmigans with their black feathers in summer and with white ones in the winter season.

"What," asked Olaf, tipping his head upward and looking at the steering star in the Northern sky, "has a hard bed and is always restless?"

"The waves of the sea," Astrid and Jon both called out at the same time.

"Here is one not to be guessed so easily," said Olaf. "It is a very old one. I had it from my grandfather, and *his* grandfather told it to him, and *he*, I have no doubt, received it in the same fashion.

> "I went from home,
> I looked on the road of roads,
> Road was above,
> Road was beneath,
> And road was in every direction."

There was a long silence, and only the waves whispered as though they were trying to tell the answer.

Then Old Olaf said, "Well, I did not guess that riddle either, so I will tell it to you, but only on condition that you both learn it so when you are very old, you may pass it on:

> "When I went from home,
> I looked on a river,
> A bird flew above me,
> His road was the air.

> "A fish swam beneath me,
> His road was the river,
> And the river—which for all Vikings
> Has been since the beginning
> The road of all roads
> That leads to the sea—
> The river flowed east and west.

> "But I stood on a bridge,
> And the road over the bridge—

The road the oxen and the horses use,
That road ran north and south.

"So there were roads in all directions,
Over me, under me, and on either hand."

"It is a good riddle," agreed Astrid, "the best I have ever heard. Do say it all over again."

While Olaf was doing this, Jon slipped away. When he came back, he brought the motherless lamb to Astrid and placed it in her lap. Almost unthinking, Astrid cradled it in her arms while she repeated the long answer to the old riddle.

After the first day was over, Astrid tried not to think any more of her black hen except to believe that Arn had found it and that his little boy was enjoying the good eggs she laid.

She and Jon enjoyed the journey to Vineland, though it seemed strange enough when the two Greenland shores were no longer to be seen, and the two boats of the Icelanders and Greenlanders were alone on the sea. But there were interesting things always: whales sometimes, and porpoises curving up out of the water, and gulls when they drew near to some island, as to Helluland—the Place of Stones—and to Markland where many trees stood, places of which Leif Ericsson had told.

There was one night of terror when the skies lowered and the waves grew mountain high, a night when Astrid and Katla huddled close together for warmth and to be out of the way of the men who were fighting desperately against the sea.

It was a night when not even the falcon slept on her perch, as Jon well knew, for twice when he stopped bailing water from the ship long enough to touch her, her head was moving restlessly and her beak was cold, for it had not been buried in the soft feathers of her shoulder.

Finally, Jon loosed the gyr from her perch and gave her to Astrid, who held her close the rest of the night. Jon had not said so, but Astrid understood that, if worse came to worst, the bird should be free to use her wings and, perchance, make some shore in safety.

But when morning drew near, the storm lessened in fury, and at dawn, it died away. Those on board drew deep breaths of thankfulness, for they knew they had come through to safety. But their companion, the second boat, had not been so blessed, for that boat had disappeared. Only Karlsefni's ship was left to continue the journey, and all that day everyone was very quiet, thinking of one after another of those who were on the lost ship.

The memories grew stronger when dusk fell once more, and they looked toward Old Olaf to change their thoughts for them. He began quietly telling brave tales of the Vikings who had ever dared the sea, who had taken the waves as their road and the sky itself as their roof.

This they had done at a time when many people had been fearful of the sea and had declared there were monsters in the waters: sea serpents and dragons and griffins.

The Northmen had answered that their boats were monsters able to triumph over any others they might meet, and they had fashioned them with heads and tails of dragons, of serpents and griffins, and set forth in them bravely, with boasting and laughter.

When they were warned that if they went too far on the waves they must come at length to the sea's edge and their boats would go tumbling off into nothingness, the

HENRY
C PITZ

Northmen had laughed louder than ever and declared that, though they had sailed far, such a thing had never yet happened.

If it did, what of that? They might find the journey through nothingness interesting. Who knew on what shores they might land, since even tumbles have an end?

It was a splendid thing, according to Olaf, who spoke now with ringing words—it was a splendid thing to steer one's boats where one would, by the sun and the stars. The Vikings had been to Ireland and Scotland; they had sailed up the rivers of Normandy and along the Blue Sea to the land of the White Christ himself.

Aye, and they had settled in the Orkneys and the Faeroes, in the Hebrides, in Iceland and in Greenland. They left the old lands and their old homes behind them and made themselves new homes in whatsoever lands to which their boats came.

Of all the tales of the Northmen, none had a braver ring than the tales of Eric the Red, who had found Greenland, and of his son, Leif, who had found the western land to which they were now going, the land he had named for its beautiful vines.

"I have not seen Vineland yet," Olaf ended, "but I think it must be the best land in all the world. And there, if all goes well, shall I earn me my freedom."

The nose of the lamb pressed against Astrid's hand, and for a moment, she remembered her little black hen.

"My hen," she said to Olaf, "would have enjoyed living in the New Land so much." And for the first time since the beginning of the long journey, Astrid's eyes were misted with tears.

"Tut, tut!" chided Olaf. "I will tell you a true thing. When the Northmen left their old homes to settle in new and strange lands, probably most of them wished they could take with them all the things they loved in the old. But they never could—not all.

"Now I shall ask you a riddle, Astrid. I myself do not know the answer, for this is a new riddle I have fashioned this moment out of the blowing of the wind, for your need. But it has an answer. Of that, I am perfectly certain. Sometime you will find that answer and tell it to me. The finding may take a long time. But if you look for it every day in Vineland, I am sure you will find it."

Astrid blinked at Olaf in amazement. Then she turned toward Jon. He, too, was staring at the old storyteller. How could Olaf ask a riddle to which he himself did not know the answer?

"Now, listen carefully!" said Olaf, as though such an admonition were necessary. "When is a pet hen not a hen?"

His eyes twinkled like sea spray in the sun, and the laughter wrinkles were a net about his eyes, and Astrid laughed, too, in spite of herself.

"How will you ever find the answer to that, Astrid?" asked Jon, when Olaf, still chuckling, left them to take his turn at the oars.

"I haven't the least idea," admitted Astrid. "Do you suppose there really is an answer?"

Katla, who had been listening, nodded. "Our father declares," she said, "that Olaf is a very wise man and has good reason for everything he says or does. So there must be an answer."

"At any rate," Astrid said, "I shall hunt for it every day."

Then she stared over the sea to where the New Land must be waiting their coming. "I do wish," she said, "we were there so I could start looking!" She repeated the riddle softly, "When is a pet hen not a hen?"

Chapter VII

The Falcon in the Land of Leif

"Vineland, at last! Vineland the Good!"

The rowers rested their oars and stood up to stare, while the women crowded among them, with some standing along the boat's right side. Astrid and Jon, by the falcon's perch, could see nothing except a line of backs. The falcon, too, was straining her neck and seemed to sense the excitement. So, on impulse, Jon unfastened her leash and lifted the bird, holding her high above his own head.

But the falcon did not relish having her wings held close

by the boy's hands, and with a quick, sharp struggle, she broke free and rose upward over the boat.

Jon was too astonished and, at the same time, too disgusted at his carelessness to utter a sound, but Astrid gave a cry of dismay. Old Olaf, looking up, saw the gyr circling. Instantly, he put his hawking whistle to his lips— the whistle which he had brought in the days of his youth from beyond the Blue Sea. The note from that whistle brought the falcon back promptly, and she settled on Jon's wrist—quickly gloved for her coming, for the glove always hung on the end of her perch.

At the same moment, silence fell over the boat, for someone had glimpsed the cross which had been raised on the Vineland beach to mark the resting place of Thorvald Ericsson, and word of this spread from mouth to mouth.

"The son slain by the strange people!" repeated Astrid, and her voice held a little note of fear.

Olaf's clear blue eyes rested on Holm's daughter for a moment before he spoke in a careless-seeming fashion. "Aye, it was a small group of men who attacked the Greenlanders. Yet these were the only people ever seen in Vineland, though Leif and his men were here for one winter, and the men of Thorvald for three. It may well be that we ourselves shall never see any of these strangers at all, for Leif believes the land is fairly large."

Astrid and Jon followed the sweep of Olaf's hand from north to south, for the others had drawn back now from the boat's side, and the two children could see the coasts stretching in either direction.

Later, they were to realize they had but begun to look at those shores. For day after day they sailed, and still there was no ending. The falcon, too, watched the land and would turn from gazing at the shore to peer into her master's face as though asking why they did not stop. She was, it appeared, anxious to test her wings over it.

And when, on an early morning, the boat passed along a beach backed by a long, level meadowland stretching back to gentle rolling country, the gyr wakened her master with a sharp cry, as though calling his attention to the fact that here surely was excellent ground from which to fly a falcon.

At least, that was how Jon interpreted the cry. "Aye," he told her, "there could be no better place."

Karlsefni, too, had been watching the ground closely. They had not gone much farther when Jon saw that he swung the tiller hard about so that the boat was drawing closer to the shore, moving, it seemed, straight toward a promontory thrusting into the sea.

As soon as the boat rounded this out-thrusting land, Karlsefni smiled, his eyes mirroring much the same pleasure as the gyr's had but a little while before. For he was looking upon a thickly wooded hill, bordered by a clear stream on one side that emptied into the sea.

Old Olaf and Holm went on shore to see whether there was a good spring on the hill. When Old Olaf returned, waving his hand and nodding even before his voice could reach them, Karlsefni gave swift orders.

"Here," he said, "we will beach the boat and build our homes. I shall name the place Straumfjord."

Jon, like the falcon, could restrain himself no longer, and a cheer left his throat, which every soul on board picked up, for they, too, were eager for the land.

Katla hurried at once for her gray goose, which she put in a basket on her arm. And Astrid, after a little hesitation, lifted the motherless lamb. But Jon left the falcon fastened by her leash on her perch while he rode The Thunderer down the gangplank and straight into some tall grass while the cows meekly followed.

Old Olaf smiled as the creatures fell eagerly to grazing. Then he called to the returning boy. "Never mind helping with the unloading here, Jon," he said. "There is another and more important task to be done first. Take the gyr back to the meadowland we passed and see whether she can bring down aught there with which to make a good broth for Gudrid. She is," he added, nodding toward Karlsefni's wife, resting under a shelter of boughs which the men had already raised, "very weary from the journey."

Then he gave Jon a single partridge he had killed with an arrow close by the spring he had found in a hollow on the hilltop. "This will be the white one's reward."

Jon's heart leaped, for he had not expected to be free to fly the falcon so soon. He started to race up the gangplank when he heard Holm saying kindly to his younger daughter, "Nay, Astrid, there is naught you can do at the moment except to keep from underfoot. Later, there will be plenty of work for all."

"Astrid!" called Jon excitedly. "Will you come with me? I am to take the falcon to the meadows and fly her for the first time in Vineland!"

Astrid nodded and went with Jon, who had already put the lure in the hunting pouch. Then, fingers trembling in their eagerness, he took the bird from her perch, set her on his wrist, and hooded her, while Astrid took the leather pouch in which to carry, in addition to the lure, whatever quarry they might bring back with them. Now she slipped the freshly killed partridge inside.

Then, with the sound of the boat's unloading growing faint in their ears, the two set out along the shore, back toward the low-lying meadows they had passed in the boat.

For a moment, Astrid's heart beat a little faster as she thought of the strange people who lived in the land. Then she looked at Jon's face, and her fear left her. "It is the best land," Jon was saying, "I have ever seen."

"Aye," agreed Astrid, but her cheeks dimpled at his words, though she did not ask him the question which came to her mind: "And how many lands have you seen?" There might, after all, be some way of understanding that this was the best land in the world-circle without having actually looked upon all others.

The grass of the meadowlands was green and lush, with clumps of reeds scattered through, and here and there a bush or a bright flower. A brook, or a small river as it seemed in places, wound carelessly through as though a silver chain had been cast from a great height upon the earth and lay as it had fallen, and an occasional tree grew along the brook's edge. Where this brook was wide, they crossed with the aid of a long pole. But Jon's and Astrid's eyes were more interested in the sky, while the gyr sat quietly, waiting for the moment when her hood should be unloosed as a signal there was work for her to do.

It was a good day for hawking. The wind was blowing inland lightly, and the moment Jon removed the hood, the falcon mounted, sailing in ever-widening circles, each one a little loftier than the last, until high in the air she was a falcon towering in her pride of place, and that place above her master's head.

Yet nothing came winging across the space beneath her, so finally Jon swung the lure to summon her back. As soon as she was down, he called her to his fist, for Astrid whispered, "I think I hear splashing in the reeds to the left."

Listening carefully, Jon could also make out faint sounds and thought there must be a hidden pool among the reeds and the cattails.

So once again he sent the falcon up, while he moved to the left of the tall, waving grasses, and Astrid moved to the right, hoping to spring the quarry. Yet Astrid was quite startled and stepped back with a thudding heart as wings rose suddenly, directly in front of her. And she blinked several times in the sunlight before she could make out the duck above her, while Jon cried excitedly to the falcon.

"Hey, gar, gar, gar!"

The king's bird needed no such call, for she, too, had seen the duck, and already her widespread wings were closing, even as Jon shouted for her to stoop.

"Hoo! Ha! Ha! Hoo! Ha! Ha!"

Down she came out of the blueness, down on her quarry like a thunderbolt. Nothing can move as fast as the gyrfalcon in her falling. Nothing, Astrid thought, with a little shudder at the sight, can strike so hard.

In the stillness she could hear the dull thud of the gyr's talons striking the neck of the hapless duck. A few feathers floated aimlessly in the air, but the duck was falling earthward while Jon jumped about wildly, yelling his approval.

The gyr, seeming to know that her work was accomplished, spread her wings and checked her own downward progress sharply. In another moment, she had veered around and was winging her way after the duck.

The quarry had fallen between Jon and Astrid, and the gyr had lighted upon it, waiting with evident satisfaction for Jon's approach. He held out his fist with a juicy morsel laid there. When the gyr sprang eagerly toward the treat, Astrid picked up the duck. As she slipped it into the pouch, she said, "It is the fattest one I have ever seen."

Only for a moment did she remember the rush of wings before her face and felt sorry that those wings would fly no more. Yet, after all, it was more important that Gudrid have food, for so Olaf had declared.

"Probably I should not fly her again so soon after the long voyage," said Jon, taking into account that his own feet were not yet steady on the ground, for the change from the rocking of the sea to the unmoving earth was not easy.

Astrid agreed, as she always did in any matter where the falcon was concerned. But Jon had no sooner uttered the words than he flung up his fist, and the gyr was once again climbing the sky.

"Wild geese!" Jon pointed exultantly, and Astrid nodded. One of these would be food indeed for Gudrid.

But the journey at sea, with only an occasional flight since leaving Greenland had, as Jon suspected, told on the gyr. And, moreover, she had not rested after bringing down her first quarry. This time she did not climb quite so high, nor was she so swift in her stooping, though the leader on which her eyes had fastened, as though scorning to single out a lesser bird, was, of course, much larger. So, while she was as certain as before in her striking, the talons did not thrust hard enough, and the head of the long vee faltered but for a moment and then quickened his flight, while the falcon was unable to check her own downward progress until she was beneath her chosen quarry.

Then she climbed more rapidly and higher, it seemed, than before, as though determination had come now to her aid. This time her stoop was swifter. The wild gander faltered, and though he still strove to save himself, he moved his wings wildly for a moment, yielded his place, and turned earthward. Even before the great bird reached the ground, the falcon had remounted, stooped, and struck a third time, and the two disappeared in the tall grasses almost at the same instant.

But Astrid did not see the end of the struggle. She was watching the rest of the wild geese and had marked how another in the flock took the leader's place as soon as he had been struck the second time. The new leader had headed the two converging lines hastily out over the sea, as though sensing that there the gyr was not likely to follow.

Since the quarry had fallen at some distance from them, Jon marked the place with his eyes, noting the sun and the top of a certain hill, before going to the falcon.

He praised her again, stroked her, and gave her the best of the partridge remaining. He and Astrid waited for her to eat this before picking up the fallen gander.

"You shall have all the breast feathers," declared Jon to Astrid, "and in time, you will have a pillow fashioned from naught but the breast down of the wild geese which my falcon shall bring you."

And then he could have bitten his tongue if, by so doing, he could have recalled the words "my falcon." For he knew from the stricken look in Astrid's eyes that she was remembering a day when they had talked of the merits of "my falcon" and "my black hen."

So, to make up for his carelessness, he sent Astrid on ahead with news of the gyr's success. "Tell Olaf," he instructed her, "that our falcon has already shown how well she will do in the land of Leif the Lucky."

Astrid was the first, too, the next morning, to bring news to Jon and Olaf. "It is a good thing we brought home food for Gudrid," she said, "for this morning, she has a newborn son. She is naming him Snorri. The Vineland colony is growing already."

Jon blinked, but Olaf sat up on his bed of fir boughs and cried out with delight, "A child newborn in a new land! That will indeed bring us luck."

Chapter VIII

Floki's Ravens to the Rescue

The first months in any new home are always busy ones,
and so Jon and Astrid found those first months in the New
Land, since there was a special need of haste for the settlers
to build their halls on the hilltop Karlsefni had chosen.

Those halls of logs were barely up and roofed over when
winter settled like a falcon's hood over the land. Even then,
there was still much to do to make the halls more livable
on the inside and to care for the cattle and sheep in the
hastily erected byre. Meanwhile, every day the men must

go out with bows and arrows and hunting spears to seek some wild creature of the land for food or to fish through the ice of the stream or out on the sea.

Olaf, however, had not forgotten before the snow fell to gather and dry the grass from the meadowland for the cattle and sheep. When winter came and any further supply was covered, he and Jon added bark stripped from the trees to their meager diet, and the cooked bones from the fish as well.

Because of the care of Karlsefni and his people and of Olaf for the cattle and sheep, all lived through the difficult season of the year without suffering and came safely into the spring. This was due in some measure to the fact that the winters in the New Land were not as severe as those in Greenland.

Yet everyone was glad when spring came early, and Old Olaf seemed happiest of all. Astrid, however, noticed there was a frequently puzzled expression on his face, particularly at the end of each day when he would stand on the hilltop and look about over Vineland, as far as he could see, and she asked him why this was.

"I cannot answer that question very well yet, Astrid," he said. "But there is a sense of something new and strange in this land, a feeling which is in the very air. Yet, try as I will, I cannot name it."

Jon could not explain what Olaf had meant when Astrid repeated his words. But they both soon forgot the strange answer in the hurry and bustle which took place as soon as it was certain that spring had come to stay.

For Karlsefni ordered that the cattle and sheep be
loaded on the small boat that they had brought with them,
trailing behind the larger one and called for that reason
the "after-boat." Then he and his men rowed them out to
a nearby island, where there was plenty of good grass, and
left them there.

Karlsefni felt it wiser to explore further along the coast
of the land to which they had come, to be certain the
strange people did not live near. So after the cattle and
sheep were cared for, the big boat was made ready, and all
from Straumfjord took their places in it once more. Katla
insisted on having her gray goose in a pen on board and a
wild gander, which had been brought down with a broken
wing, which Katla had likewise cared for.

The journey along the shore was delightful. And, what
was more important, no sign at all of any other inhabitants
in Vineland was found. After Karlsefni thought they had
explored far enough, they sailed into the mouth of a river.
And as the boat moved with the tide, the river widened
unexpectedly until it seemed as though the boat were
riding in a wide and beautiful lake. Here the colonists
decided to remain for a time, for the hunting and fishing
were good. Karlsefni named the place Landlocked Bay.

And here Olaf discovered wild grapevines growing, the
fragrance in their tiny, unseen blossoms giving promise
of good harvest. Olaf likewise discovered wild grain, not
yet ready for gathering. So it was decided that Old Olaf
and another should remain at Landlocked Bay to gather
the grapes and the grain when these both should be ripe,

while the rest would return to the halls at Straumfjord to carry on the summer's work, filling the storehouse and completing their halls.

"To say naught of flying the falcon after her molting is over," Jon remarked to Astrid.

Astrid agreed, but she did not tell even Jon of her relief that no strange people had been seen in the land. She believed that on her return, she would feel much safer at Straumfjord.

On the journey back, a raven from the south flew over them and came down for a moment on the boat's edge to rest before flying on straight toward the land.

"It was as black as my hen," said Astrid wistfully, following its flight with her eyes.

And Jon, with instant understanding, said cheerfully, "Perhaps it is one of Floki's ravens."

So, as he had known she would, Astrid made him tell her the tale of Floki, of how in the old days Floki had set forth from Norway with three birds in his boat to find the new land which Gard, a fisherman, had claimed to have come upon in the sea.

Floki had let one raven and then another free, but these had flown around for a little and returned to Floki's ship. But when Floki freed the last raven, she rose high and flew off in a straight line. So Floki followed the raven and came thus to Iceland, which some called the Land of the White Shirt because of the ice which covered some parts of it the year round.

"I had almost forgotten that tale," said Katla when he finished speaking.

"Never forget the old tales," called Holm, "for they are the stepping stones in the Northmen's journey across the sea—the tale of Floki, and of Eric, and of Leif the Lucky, who found the land where we now dwell."

"Aye," agreed Karlsefni. And he added, "We shall see our halls and sleep on our own benches this night."

Karlsefni spoke true words, for they came that night to Straumfjord and found everything as they had left it, except for the cattle and sheep. These were much fatter, and there were even two newcomers among them on the island, twin lambs born in the New Land, even as Snorri Karlsefnisson had been.

"Tomorrow," called Jon happily to Astrid, "we shall go to the meadowland and fly the falcon. I shall pull her out early on her block while I hurry to do all my other tasks."

And so he did, and hurried too much as he later knew only too well, remembering how Olaf always said, "That which is done well is done fast enough."

Perhaps Astrid might have avoided the tragedy had she not been busy aiding Katla, and only when she heard Jon's call did she come to the doorway of Holm's hall. Yet when she was there, Jon said no word. He was staring up at the falcon's empty block, and then up into an equally empty sky. It was Astrid who said, rather than asked, the two words, "The falcon!"

Jon turned toward her, and his face was miserable. "I must have been careless in tying the leash," he managed at last.

Astrid knew well why Jon was so alarmed, for a falcon flying loose with the leash attached to her jesses is in great

danger. The leash may tangle in a treetop and be caught
and even wound about a branch so that the falcon is
imprisoned. And, in the end, she may die of hunger and be
found hanging head down in the air. While, if such a bird is
blessed enough not to be so caught by the leash, there is but
little hope that, thus handicapped, she can fend for herself.

So Astrid called back to Katla with no hesitation, "The falcon is lost, and I am going with Jon to find it."

Jon took Old Olaf's hawking whistle from the shelf and the lure attached to the long walrus rope, together with a piece of a freshly killed rabbit with which to bait it. Even though the falcon might not hear either his call or that of the ivory whistle, she might glimpse the wide-swinging lure, for the falcon can see for very great distances—much farther than man.

But though they hunted all day, going out even to the meadowland and then back through the thick wood which, after one passed first through a swampland and then an open glade, stretched far in back and to the left of Straumfjord, they saw no sign of the bird.

Jon wished he had fastened the little silver bells to her feet above the jesses, where she usually wore them, for he might have heard these from a distance, especially had the falcon been caught and imprisoned by her leash, for her struggles would have set the bells to ringing wildly. But he had removed the bewits to which the bells were attached only the day before.

Yet it was as useless to bewail their lack now as to bewail his carelessness. All he and Astrid could do was to search as far and as thoroughly as possible, to search and watch the skies for a glimpse of the wide wings above them, and to listen for any unusual behavior on the part of the Vineland birds, particularly the ravens.

Once, to be sure, they did hear the black birds making a great racket, as ravens always do when they come upon a hawk in the trees. When they heard such a cawing, Astrid and Jon hurried as fast as they could to the spot, only to glimpse a gray owl winging silently out of the thick branches of a pine and hastening across to an even thicker place in the wood, followed by a long, trailing line of the cawing birds. It was a sight to see, but not, alas, that sight which they wanted most to look upon.

Once again they had hope when, far off to the east, Jon saw the welcoming circle of a great hawk. "It is the falcon!" he shouted with relief, yet the last word lagged a little on his lips, for there was something about the manner in which the newcomer circled which seemed slightly different, and after a bit, he cried out in disappointment and astonishment.

"Nay, it is not the falcon, Astrid. It is a white gyr-tiercel. Of that, I am certain."

He was certain of another thing, too, though he did not speak this last certainty aloud. But had the falcon been anywhere near and able to fly, she would have been brought into the sky by the sight of the second hawk, the male of her own breed. When only the tiercel continued to soar in solitary splendor among the clouds and finally disappeared toward the east, Jon was more fearful than ever that the whitest falcon of all must have been caught and imprisoned by her own leash. Surely, Eric the Red would never have entrusted him with the king's bird had he known to what an end it would come.

Almost frantic with his fear for the gyr and paying little heed to his steps, after he had swung his lure vainly in every open space he could find, Jon hastened deeper and deeper into the wood, believing the bird must be caught in some tree.

Astrid followed as best she could after him. It seemed to her that his eyes must have pierced through every leaf of every tree, so anxiously did they seek the lost falcon, though the day was drawing to an end, the clouds were thick, and the very air strangely damp.

Astrid's feet were hurting, her arms were scratched, and she was tired and hungry. However, she made no complaint until Jon, looking back impatiently for her, caught sight of the expression on her face and heard her little gasp of distress as she stumbled over a twisting root.

"Let's stop and gather some of these berries," he suggested, pointing to some half-hidden on their vines in the moss at his feet, berries which had remained red and sweet through the winter. Though they were small, they helped still their hunger a little.

"I feel better," said Astrid at length. "But look, Jon, at the fog settling above us."

Jon knew quick dismay at the sight of the tops of the trees already shrouded in white, branch after branch disappearing in swirls of soft mist.

"Perhaps," ventured Astrid, "we should go home now. We can look again tomorrow. Many times, you know, falcons have been lost for days before they were found."

"Aye," agreed Jon. "We will go back." He glanced about him carelessly at first, and then his expression became intent, little lines marking his forehead.

"Have you any idea, Astrid," he asked, "which way the meadowland or the hill lies from here?"

Astrid stared at him. "I?" she asked in turn. "Of course not." And then firmly, "You will know after a little, Jon. You can find the way. I know you can. Though it would be much easier if you had one of Floki's ravens to guide you."

"I need a guide of some sort," he admitted. "But until I can decide what to do, let us find a stone or a log and sit quietly." He was recalling how often Olaf had told tales of Northmen who had wearied themselves out wandering in circles. Unless one knew directions, it was better to stay in one place and wait until the sun or the stars could be glimpsed.

They could still see a little, and they made their way toward a white stone which stood in front of some thick bushes. Jon put out his hand to thrust the bushes back to make more room, and as he did so, a strange bird suddenly flew from the bushes with great protesting. Half running on long, ungainly legs, half flying on wings, which seemed somehow equally ungainly, it disappeared in the foggy wood.

"We must have disturbed her spring nesting," said Jon. Bending, he ran his hand along the moss on either side of the stone. Sure enough, he found eggs, seven of them, still warm from the bird's breast. He took two and gave them to Astrid, who slipped them in her kerchief which she tied to her belt.

Then they seated themselves on the stone to wait. Jon kept thinking about how foolish he had been. Now the falcon was lost, and he and Astrid were lost, too—three

Greenlanders lost in Vineland, where the strange people dwelt. It was the first time that fear of these people had come to him, and he put the thought aside almost at once.

This was a good land, this Vineland, as good a land, nay, better, than Floki had found with his ravens. If only, as Astrid had said, he too had a raven, a guide of some sort.

All of a sudden, he started to his feet. Overhead he caught a sound, the sound of one wild duck calling to another. And, after a little, the duck was answered by another in the distance and yet another.

Jon laughed aloud. "Come on," he said, "can't you hear the ravens of Floki?"

"Hear what?" asked Astrid, rising obediently.

"Floki's ravens," answered Jon.

"I hear birds, but they sound like ducks to me," she said.

"Nevertheless, if you had not spoken of Floki, I would not have caught their signal. Now I know the way to go. I have only to follow their calling. For at this season, in storm or night time, they always go—Oh, wait, Astrid, and learn for yourself. Perhaps it's another riddle."

And though the fog was as thick as ever, Jon's steps were certain. Only now and then, he must stop to listen until he heard another duck calling out of the fog above him.

Then Astrid heard something else—the breaking of the surf on the seashore.

"The sea," she said.

"Aye," answered Jon. "I have been wondering when you would hear it."

"So that is the answer," said Astrid. "I must have seen

ducks turning seaward before dusk or the storm as often as you, yet I have no memory of it. Well, all we must do now is follow the shoreline," she said with relief.

"Aye, it will be easy to find our way home now," he agreed, "for I know we must have come out west of the hill, since we have crossed no meadowland."

And so it proved, though it was quite late when the two came to Straumfjord and to the door of Karlsefni's hall, where they stood staring as though the fire were a star beyond which they were beholding something quite marvelous—as indeed they were. For there, on her padded perch by Jon's bed, sat the falcon, mantling and preening her feathers.

When the welcome of the pair was over, and they had explained how they had found their way, Jon asked Holm about the falcon.

He smiled and said that Katla knew more about the bird than he. So Katla told how, just before the fog closed in, the white bird had come out of the mist, racing it seemed before it, to settle straight on her block.

Katla had called her father, and Holm had brought the falcon inside Karlsefni's hall. Now he said briefly, "All that was lost is found."

At the word *found*, Astrid remembered the eggs tied in her kerchief, and after everyone had looked at them and none in the hall could name them, she gave them to Gudrid.

"I shall put them in this basket," said Gudrid. "In the morning, I shall cook them, and you two can learn whether they are good to eat."

But in the morning, the basket was empty. And when Gudrid asked Jon if he had taken them, he replied, "Are the eggs lost, too?"

His eyes were twinkling, and Gudrid did not question him further. After all, if he and Astrid did not choose to eat the eggs they had found, that was their affair.

Chapter IX

A Riddle Answered, a Riddle Asked

After Karlsefni had brought the settlers back to
Straumfjord, everyone set about the summer's work in
earnest. The women gathered herbs and berries to dry for
the winter. They washed the wool taken from the sheep
for the winter's spinning and weaving. They gathered salt,
too, by carrying buckets of sea water to depressions in
the rocks where the sun licked up the water and left the
precious salt.

The men still spent much time hunting and fishing.

For, besides their present needs, meat and fish must be dried for the storehouse. And while procuring these, they explored the land at the same time, learning where all the bounty of the surrounding country could be found: good nuts for the eating, berries, and wild herbs.

To Astrid and Jon fell the task of minding the cattle and the sheep, which had been brought in from the island. They grazed now, for the most part, in a little open valley in back of the hill where the halls were built, a hidden and unexpected glade which could be reached by a single path, since a strip of marshland lay between it and the hill.

On the way with their charges to this glade, Jon stopped long enough, the morning after they had been lost, to slip the two eggs he and Astrid had brought back with them underneath Katla's gray goose, which had recently decided to bring up a family in the New World.

The goose hissed a little, but the minute Jon withdrew his hand, she had spread her gray wings a trifle wider, moved the eggs beneath her into position with her feet, and settled down, looking, Astrid declared, more comfortable than before.

Then, as one day piled upon another, both Astrid and Jon forgot about the eggs.

But one afternoon Katla had news when Astrid returned. "The gray goose has hatched most of her eggs," she said, "though one of them is the strangest gosling I have ever seen."

When Astrid began to rock back and forth at the sight of that gosling, Katla inquired anxiously, "Do you think it is sick or something?"

"It is you who are the goose," answered Astrid. "*That* isn't!"

"Then what is it?" demanded Katla.

"What is it?" repeated Astrid, a little foolishly, Katla thought.

Just then Jon came back from the sheep byre, and Astrid called, "Jon, come here! Katla's goose has hatched—has hatched—Well, Katla wants to know what she *has* hatched."

"I don't know," said Jon, looking at the fledgling. "I—really—I haven't the least idea." Then he joined his laughter with Astrid's.

Not until the next day, when the second egg hatched another strange fledgling, did they tell Katla what had really happened. And though Astrid's sister was amused, she was also a little anxious. She wasn't at all sure how the wild birds would fit into the family of the gray goose.

Neither, it seemed, was the gray goose! But she did the best she could with what nature had presented her—though when, a little later, it came to the matter of urging the two long-legged ones into the water, she found herself in difficulties. They refused to obey, but instead stayed cheerfully on the shore, scratching in the dirt and eating wild seeds.

"I do wish Olaf would return and see what we have," said Astrid more than once.

"He would probably be better pleased if you had found him some honey bees and some honey," reminded Katla. "'Honey,' he has said often, 'is the one thing which this land lacks.'"

"I know," said Astrid. "We have looked and looked, Jon and I, for the honeybee of which he has told us, but we haven't seen one. The only strange things we have found are—"

She suddenly stopped speaking and danced around and around like a small whirlwind. "I have it," she cried at last, breathlessly, "I have it!"

"Honey?" asked Katla.

"Katla! Katla! You never do understand what I am thinking about. It's the answer to Olaf's riddle, of course."

"Riddle?" asked Katla, more bewildered than ever.

"Really, Katla," said Astrid, "you are a goose, after all." And that was every word she would say.

Not even Jon could persuade her to explain. And Jon had learned from experience that Astrid could keep secrets.

"When Olaf comes home, I will tell you," she promised, her eyes dancing. "But I must tell him first, just to be certain I am right."

And so when, late that autumn on an early morning, Jon saw the boat Karlsefni had taken back to Landlocked Bay coming with spread sail toward Straumfjord, he hurried to call Astrid.

"The boat is coming with Olaf," he said. "Shall we meet him?"

"Aye," replied Astrid. "But wait, I must go for Katla." And though Katla was busy with her sweeping, it did not take any urging to have her cast aside the broom of green twigs and hurry down to the shore with them to meet the ship.

"We've dried grapes," called Olaf when he saw them, "and plenty of grain for your porridge this winter, to say naught of the most wonderful wine ever poured in a drinking horn or a silver cup from Norway, wine which I brewed at Landlocked Bay from the wild grapes."

"Good! Good!" called Astrid. And then she added triumphantly, "We've something, too."

"As fine as what I have brought?" demanded Olaf, leaning toward them over the boat's edge.

"Aye, as fine."

"So? Then I must hasten to see it," he said. And he leaped like a boy over the boat's edge and came wading through the last of the breakers to the shore, giving Astrid a handful of the ripe grain he had brought home.

"Where is this fine thing?" he demanded.

"Wait a little," Astrid answered. And then, because she couldn't keep her secret any longer, she blurted out, "You see, I have found it!"

"You have found it?" repeated Olaf. He slowed his pace and looked down at her. He was wiser than Katla or Jon, for he said, "Have you now? Well, when *is* a pet hen not a hen?"

Astrid lifted his hand to her cheek. "Come, and I'll show you." She dimpled.

And she led Olaf, while Jon and Katla followed, to the side of the brook. There was the old gray goose swimming over the pebbles with her goslings strung out in a line behind her. But on shore, two of the strangest birds turned at once and came running to her on long, thin legs.

Astrid held out the handful of wild grain Olaf had given her, just as nearly every day, before going to the glade, she had held out a handful of wild seeds of some sort to the fledglings. Both birds bent at once to her hand. After the seeds were gone, one of the birds tried to spread its tail feathers, which were growing a little longer every day. They made a bronze fan, and the bird seemed very proud, for it strutted about.

"There is the answer, Olaf," said Astrid. "A pet hen is not a pet hen when it is a Vineland bird. See!" And as Astrid walked up the path, the curious birds followed close at her heels.

"Aye," agreed Olaf. "You have found the answer. When one leaves the things one loves in the Old Land, one finds other things to love in the New. That is what I meant when I fashioned my riddle for you.

"I knew well enough you would find something to love in Vineland, but I did not know what. But all riddles have answers, that I knew, even though I did not know what the answer itself would be."

He studied the birds and wrinkled his brow, trying hard to recall something nearly forgotten. "I never saw a peacock," he said at length, "but I have heard of them from others. They are proud birds, and the cocks likewise spread their tails like a fan, though the hens are modest creatures."

"Then my bird with the spreading tail must be the Vineland cock," declared Astrid, "while the one which does not spread its feathers must be the Vineland hen."

"Goggle, goggle, goggle," answered the Vineland cock.

So that was how Olaf's first riddle was answered in Vineland. But before winter came, he and all the others at

Straumfjord were asking another and even more important riddle, and had no certainty as to what the answer might be. But everyone knew a great deal would depend on it.

This riddle was asked for the first time on the day Old Olaf met with an accident. He had gone out hunting early in the morning, as was his custom, and Jon, sometime later when he was feeding the falcon perched on his fist, heard him calling.

"Boats!" came Olaf's cry. "Boats coming from the south!" And then, "Can you hear me?"

"Aye," responded Jon, making a trumpet of his hands. "Aye, Olaf, I hear."

"Tell Karlsefni," came back Olaf's voice with relief in its tones.

"Aye," called Jon, and he turned to Karlsefni, who, having heard Jon's shouting, was already at his side, while Gudrid with Snorri in her arms was standing in the open door.

"The strange people are coming, I think," said Karlsefni to his wife. "Olaf has seen them and called a warning, which Jon was lucky enough to hear."

Gudrid nodded. Her face was calm as she said quietly, "Doubtless they come in friendship and peace. Take the white shield and hold it high." And she set the child on the floor and went to take the peace shield from its place on the wall.

Astrid, who had slipped out to Jon's side at the sound of his calling, felt her heart beneath her kirtle beating hard and fast with her old fear—*the strange people, the people who had killed the son of Eric the Red!*

Soon everyone on the hill could see the small boats coming around a jutting headland that hid the south from the eyes of those on the hill. There was a great number of boats, and in them were men waving what seemed to be staves. These staves moved from east to west as the sun moves. That was, in itself, a good sign, Karlsefni decided, since men of good will always do things in the same fashion as the sun moves. Does not a man measure his land by burning the boundaries with fire always from east to west? The king travels always with the sun through his kingdom.

As the settlers stood thus, waiting, everything and everyone on the hill was very quiet. Suddenly, out of the wood, they could hear Olaf calling again.

"Karlsefni," he was saying, "can you hear me?"

"Aye, Olaf, we hear," answered Karlsefni.

"When the strangers are close," called Olaf, "bid Jon take up the falcon and launch her from the hilltop."

"That I will do," answered Karlsefni, though his voice was puzzled, while Jon, who had set the bird upon her block, at once slipped the glove on his left hand again and took her up.

The boats came nearer and nearer and finally beached on the shore at the foot of the hill. The men who were in them jumped from the boats and drew them up on the sand. Then, in little groups, the strangers stood, staring upward at the halls built on the hilltop, staring at the men and women gathered before those halls, and looking curiously at Karlsefni's uplifted shield, white in the sunlight.

"Now," Karlsefni told Jon with a nod, "go in front of us so that the strangers can see you clearly."

And this Jon did with the hooded falcon riding on his fist.

"Yonder comes a raven," cried Karlsefni, pointing. "Fly the falcon!"

So Jon slipped the hood with its tuft of feathers from the falcon's head and cast her into the wind. She circled up and up into the sky. Every stranger on the beach threw back his head and craned his neck to watch her.

It seemed as though the gyr knew she had an audience, for her pitch was a higher one than she usually made. And when she stooped, the falcon's aim was so swift and certain that the raven never knew what happened.

Then straight to the boy's outstretched hand came the bird, bearing her quarry with her, bound tight in her talons.

Jon took the dead raven from her with his right hand and handed it to Karlsefni, who held it high, as though displaying it to the watchers on the beach.

They looked from the dead bird toward one another, and an approving murmur came up to those on the hilltop.

Then again out of the wood came Olaf's voice. "Have ye flown the falcon?"

"Aye," answered Karlsefni.

"Then bid Jon ride The Thunderer before them," came Olaf's next order.

Karlsefni looked even more bewildered, but he declared, "Olaf must have a good reason for what he is asking."

So Jon set the falcon on her block, and Astrid slipped the swivel into the jesses and then through the unknotted end of the leash and tied the leash to the staple on the block, using the falconer's knot and being very careful to make it fast. She had no more than finished her task when Jon, who had gone in back of the halls for the bull, came riding The Thunderer around Karlsefni's hall and in front of the group of settlers.

Astrid was always filled with astonishment when Jon rode the creature, for The Thunderer would allow no one

else even to approach him without lowering his horns threateningly, though never, as far as Astrid knew, had he harmed a human being.

Because of the way she herself felt, she was not in the least surprised that the visitors on the beach looked astounded at the sight. Some of the more timid even began to edge their boats back into the sea.

Neither did Jon miss the expressions on the faces looking up at him. Suddenly he started The Thunderer down the hill and directly toward the huddled group on the beach, guiding the creature by his horns.

The turn of events was altogether too much for the strangers. With one accord, they bent over their boats and launched them hurriedly. Then, taking up their long staves, in no time at all they had rounded the headland and disappeared. Save for the marks of their feet on the sand of the seashore, no one could have told they had really been at Straumfjord.

But Astrid was already asking herself the questions, "When will they come again, and will they be friendly?" She knew there was no one who could answer.

Karlsefni watched until the last boat had disappeared, and then he put his hands to his lips and called to Olaf.

"Why do you not come home?" he demanded.

"I can't," called back the old man. "I have broken my leg, for I caught it in a root and stumbled when I hurried to tell you of what I saw on the sea."

Karlsefni at once ordered the men to make a litter of skins tied to small saplings. Then, with Jon, they went for Olaf and brought him home. It was a bad break, and he was suffering much, but Gudrid, who was skilled at nursing, put the ends of the broken bone together and bound the leg with strips of wadmal.

"If you will remain quiet," she promised, "in time, the leg will be as good as new."

Olaf's eyes brightened at the promise, and then, from his bench, he demanded that he be told all that had taken place. When he learned how the strangers had murmured at the sight of the falcon returning to the boy's fist with her quarry and how they had retreated hurriedly to their boats at the approach of The Thunderer with Jon on his back, Olaf was pleased. He declared it was his opinion that the strangers had been greatly impressed. When they returned, he thought they would be friendly and not risk warring against men who could control even the birds of the air and the beasts of the earth.

Karlsefni hoped that Old Olaf was right. And he said, "Now do I understand why you asked these things of Jon, though I myself would not have thought to do it. We are in your debt, Olaf, and men in debt do not live easily, nor can they expect good luck to continue with them. Will you not," he went on, "let us hold a freedom ale for you, and by so doing, pay our debt and ensure ourselves luck?"

Olaf looked troubled, for Northmen and descendants of Northmen put much store by luck. But finally he shook his head. "Nay," he said, "I must purchase my own freedom ale with my own gold."

Neither would he take a gold mark for what he had done, for he insisted he had but served himself as well

as the others. Then he changed the subject and asked
Karlsefni how the strangers had looked, for he had seen
them only from a great distance.

"They are slender," explained Karlsefni, "and their hair
is black and straight, their cheekbones high, while their
eyes seemed small. Yet there was something about their
appearance which I did not like. I am not at all certain how
our dealings with them may turn out. But since we must
have a name for them, I shall call them Skraelings."

The word seemed to fit, and after that, everyone at
Straumfjord spoke of them as *Skraelings*.

Chapter X

The Mystery in the Vineland Glade

The summer was passing swiftly in the little open valley in back of the halls where the cattle and sheep grazed, and where Astrid and Jon spent much of their time watching them.

Early in the spring, the falcon had been there, too. At first, Jon carried her on his fist every morning and sent her up for short flights above the glade, calling her back by the swinging lure or occasionally by his own voice or whistle. But for the most part, when he flew her for quarry, he took her out to the meadowland.

Then one morning, at Olaf's suggestion, Jon loosed the falcon at the same time as he himself left the hill, and the bird followed him, even though the treetops often hid him from her sight.

Finally, Jon set forth, leaving the falcon on her block by Olaf's side. When Jon was out of sight, Olaf took the bird on his own fist, and not until he heard the notes from the ivory hawking whistle did Olaf cast her off. As they had both hoped, the bird mounted at once above the halls and with no hesitation winged toward the glade, where she settled with evident delight on Jon's fist.

But after the molting began, the falcon remained on the hill, quiet for the most part on her perch, which Olaf set outside and over which Jon had contrived a little tent of skins, open at one side for the sun to shine in but closed at night. Molting, Olaf declared, was not easy for any falcon. He said it robbed them of vigor and strength. If due care were not taken at the time, they were prone to develop various weaknesses. There are many secrets in caring for gyrfalcons, especially when they have been taken to warmer lands than that of their birth. But Old Olaf knew them all. The most important, he always said, concerned their care in the summer season.

Oil from crushed snails was needed with which to drench the falcon's food before giving it to her. One morning while Astrid was digging some herbs for Gudrid, Jon was wandering about the glade searching for snails. Suddenly he saw the shadow of wings moving over the grass at his feet. And, looking up, he glimpsed for a moment the tiercel, the very one he felt sure he had seen on the day the falcon had been lost. The tiercel also was molting, for there were gaps in his wings where some flight feathers were missing, but he must still find his own food as best he could, though now, Jon thought, he must depend on small quarry and even nestlings.

Jon remained standing for several minutes with his head back and his hands on his hips, hoping that the tiercel would circle once more over the glade. So absorbed was he in his watching that he missed Astrid's quick gasp of dismay and fear; missed, too, the first sight of the lone Skraeling.

The Skraeling was a girl about Astrid's own size, and Astrid had come upon her suddenly at a turn of the path. For a moment, the girls had remained staring at each other, both being too astonished to move, although Astrid alone had given a gasp at the unexpected meeting.

Then from the bundle on the Skraeling girl's back had come a pitiful wailing cry, such as Jon and Astrid had heard the wee Snorri give during the first months after his birth, a cry which Gudrid had explained was one of hunger.

Jon lowered his head at the sound. Some instinct made him make all his moves slowly, though his eyes moved fast enough as he took in the sight of Astrid, white with fear, facing the Skraeling whom he could see was equally afraid. The Skraeling girl, however, was trying very hard not to show how she felt. Keeping her widened eyes on Astrid, she was reaching a piece of partly chewed meat back toward the head bobbing over one shoulder, and the child seized this hopefully.

"We have better food than that for a baby," said Jon, and his voice was low and gentle. Even in the midst of her own fear, Astrid was reminded of times in Greenland when Jon and Olaf had caught wild peregrines in the falconer's net. It was similar also to the voice he used when, for some reason or other, the whitest of all the falcons was disturbed and he quieted her.

As he spoke, the Skraeling seemed to realize for the first time that there was a third person in the glade, and Jon could see her straighten and cast a sidelong glance at the nearest thicket, as though planning to flee.

But before she could do this, Jon turned his back on both girls and walked toward one of the cows picketed in the glade. "Come, Astrid," he said, still speaking softly. "We have food for the child here."

Astrid at once turned and followed him. When the Skraeling saw them both moving away from her, toward the side of the tethered creatures, her tenseness seemed to leave her. She hesitated for a moment, then, taking a step or two forward, stood still at the glade's edge, watching.

Astrid seated herself on the stone as Jon suggested and began to milk the cow into the drinking horn which Jon had taken from his belt, where it had been held fast by a hook riveted to the top.

When the horn was quite full and even spilling over, Jon raised it to his own lips and drank, smacking his lips together as though it tasted very good. For so he had noticed Gudrid had sometimes lured Snorri into tasting new and strange food. Then Jon handed the horn to Astrid. "Drink, too," he said.

So Astrid, just beginning to understand what Jon was planning, drank and smacked her lips. Then Jon knelt by the cow again, and the horn was refilled.

"You carry it to her, Astrid," he suggested.

"Nay—" she began, but Jon did not seem to hear. He still held the horn toward her. "The baby is hungry."

By this time, the other girl also seemed to have lost some of her fear. She waited quietly and a little curiously. When Astrid, standing as far from her as she could, reached out the horn, the Skraeling hesitated only a moment before taking it. She held it to her lips and sipped doubtfully.

In another moment, with a single hand, she had managed to slip the baby from her back and was standing the curious framework, in which it was fastened, upright on the ground, while she held the horn full of milk toward the crying child.

"That is not the way," said Astrid. And, kneeling beside the Skraeling, she lifted the baby, framework and all, and placed it across her own knees. Here, raising the baby's head with one hand, with the other Astrid held the horn to its lips while Jon watched. Old Olaf could have told from his face, could he have seen it, that Jon was a little astonished at Holm's younger daughter, although it was also evident that he quite approved.

When the horn was emptied, Astrid gave the child back to the Skraeling and came across the glade to refill it. At length, the baby had enough and turned its face sleepily away, so Astrid offered the remaining milk in the horn to the strange girl to drink.

The Skraeling gulped it down, eying Astrid the while. Finally, her fear was too much for her. She suddenly jumped to her feet, clutched the baby to her, and, carefully avoiding both the grazing cattle and sheep, ran swiftly along the edge of the glade until she was as far from both Astrid and Jon as possible.

Then she paused and looked back as though half expecting she was being followed. But Astrid remained sitting in the same position she had been in when the Skraeling baby was lying on her, and Jon had not moved.

Following an impulse, Astrid made a little friendly gesture with her hand, and, to the astonishment of Jon, the Skraeling responded in like manner. In another instant, she parted the bushes and disappeared.

"That baby was starving, Jon," Astrid said, when no further sign came of the girl's presence, "and the girl was hungry, too."

"They were Skraelings," said Jon, seeking to test her feelings with the word.

"They were hungry," repeated Astrid. "I should like to help them. I could borrow one of Katla's kettles," she went on, "and we could leave it on a rock with milk in it."

But Jon was perplexed. "How do you know the girl is alone, Astrid?" he asked at length.

"I never thought of that," admitted Astrid, and she looked hurriedly about. But the glade seemed unchanged.

A butterfly wavered over a flower. A small striped creature was running up and down a tree. A raven cawed from a dead limb overhead.

"What do you think we had better do, Jon?" asked Astrid, as he made no suggestion.

"I believe we had better tell Olaf," he answered. "He will know what is best. After all, we do have to think of the others at Straumfjord."

"But if he says we may, I shall borrow the kettle," persisted Astrid.

To this, Jon was willing to agree. And surprisingly enough, that was just what Old Olaf did.

When the two came to him with their report, he had listened quietly from the bench outside Karlsefni's hall, where he sat most of the time with his injured leg outstretched.

Not until they had finished did Olaf speak. Then he declared, "It is indeed a strange story you have brought me this day, but I think we should keep this a secret between us until we find out why the girl and the baby are there. If they had not both been so hungry, I would be certain it was a trap of some sort. Yet Karlsefni and the men have been out every day and have brought no word of strangers or signs of strangers in the neighborhood. And if these were about in any number, they must have done so."

He pulled at his beard for a time and then spoke further. "Aye," he said, "it may be that it *is* a trap and that danger threatens. But if so, you are children of Northmen and can face with courage whatever may come to pass. Yet, after this, let Jon not leave the hill without the hawking whistle. And if he sees danger closing about, let him blow the whistle once or twice, if possible, and I shall take care that those on this hilltop are warned.

"On the other hand, it is possible that the girl is lost or has strayed from a larger group. You try and follow her, Jon, and find out if she is indeed alone."

So the next morning Jon departed with the hawking whistle and Astrid with Katla's smallest iron kettle, which she had secretly borrowed.

Before Astrid finished her milking, for this was work which women always did, Jon murmured that he could see the Skraeling near the place where she had been the day before.

Holm's daughter tilted her head against the cow's smooth side, to show that she had heard and to enable her to steal a glance in the same direction.

Then Jon began whistling a song he had heard Gudrid sing the past winter to the small Snorri, while Gudrid rocked him back and forth in a cradle made from the trunk of a Vineland tree. As he had hoped, the sound seemed to give the Skraeling confidence, for she stepped boldly forth and stood in the path, waiting and ready for the good food which she could see falling in a thin, white stream from between Astrid's fingers.

Astrid took both kettle and drinking horn with her when she moved toward the Skraeling and, putting the kettle on the ground, held out her arms for the child. The Skraeling hesitated only long enough to peer into the kettle, but the sight of the whiteness there won her over.

Yet it seemed that she would snatch the child from Astrid when Jon, too, came in that direction. At her first movement, however, Jon had paused and held out toward her the package of cheese he had brought.

It was a giving gesture, even as Astrid's proffer of the horn had been the day before, and the Skraeling hesitated. Then Jon said kindly, as though he were certain she would understand the tone if not the words, "Aye, it is for you." And he held the package to his lips and pretended he was eating from it.

The Skraeling reached for the gift. And, as the bark of its own accord unfolded, the girl raised both hands to her lips as Jon had done and began to eat the curd cheese. It was plain from the instant delight on her face that she liked the taste of the curious food very much. Yet, when the cheese was about gone, she stopped and looked at the remaining curds longingly before folding the bark over and slipping the package into a skin pouch which she wore over one shoulder.

Jon noted her action with care, for he knew he must report to Olaf that the Skraeling was evidently taking part of the cheese to someone, unless, of course, she was saving it to eat later.

As on the day before, the girl skirted the glade as far from Jon and Astrid as possible and disappeared. But as she turned, she and Astrid exchanged the gesture of friendliness; and right afterward, Astrid set the kettle, with the milk still covering the bottom, on a rock, then pointed to it and then to the girl at the wood's edge. The Skraeling looked at the kettle and nodded. Then, as quickly as before, she disappeared.

When later that morning Jon went to the place where they had last seen the stranger, he could not even find her footprints.

The falcon's molting went on, and though Jon always spent some time with the bird early every morning, talking to her and calling her from the perch to his hand, he did not miss her in the glade as much as he had expected. He was too busy these days trying to find out where the Skraeling disappeared with the baby every morning after he and Astrid had brought them food.

Yet, for a long time, the only footprints he made out clearly were those the Skraeling left by the Vineland rock. He found no footprints of any other Skraeling, no other footprints in the glade at all, save those which he and Astrid and the cattle and sheep made.

Every morning the Skraeling girl came for the food, and never did she eat all that was given her. Part of it was always put into her pouch and carried away. Every night Astrid left some milk in the kettle, which she stood on the rock, yet the milk was never there in the morning. Instead, the kettle was empty and placed upside down, with the drinking horn slipped in under it.

Then—and Olaf thought this was a good sign—they began to find by the drinking horn little gifts which the Skraeling left: a handful of beechnuts, and other nuts which Jon and Astrid, and Olaf as well, had never seen. Or it might be a wild fruit of some sort, or some berries wrapped in leaves. And once the girl came, bringing in her hand a beautiful arrowhead, white quartz tipped with pink, which she handed to Astrid and stood back, evidently expecting a gift for herself in return.

Astrid was perplexed, for she had nothing with her to give, and she half turned to Jon to ask what she should do. The Skraeling, as though sensing her thoughts, pointed to the braided red cloth from Norway which Astrid wore as a band about her head to hold her hair in place.

Astrid smiled, untied the ends of the band, and gave it to the Skraeling, who fastened it about her own head in the same fashion as Astrid had worn it, reaching her fingers up to pat it every now and then, and appearing to be very proud of the gift.

That day when the Skraeling went away, she carried with her not only half the boiled porridge which Jon had brought her, but the drinking horn itself was filled with white milk. It was clear, perfectly clear, that she was carrying the milk as well as the porridge to some other person.

By this time, Olaf felt confident that there must be only one other person, for from Jon and Astrid's observations, it seemed that the girl always divided evenly whatever was given her.

Yet, try as he would, Jon could not find out where the girl went when she left the glade, nor to whom she was taking the food. Once or twice, as time went on, he did come upon one or two of the stranger-girl's footprints, but not those of any other person.

Astrid and Jon and Old Olaf kept their secret well. By all three of them saving a bit from their own food each day, no one noticed, and they were able to give a package of food daily to the girl. Whatever the mystery of the Vineland glade might be, Olaf felt that now it must be followed to its ending.

He examined with care every gift from the girl that Jon and Astrid brought back from the glade. Once it was a few strange roots that Olaf did not know but which he was fairly certain must be good to eat. Again, it was a handful of strange kernels, grain of some sort, bright in color as gold itself.

As Jon searched about the glade for the Skraeling's trail, more than once he felt certain that the stranger-girl herself was watching him. Twice he thought he heard a little chuckle of amusement, though afterward he decided it must have been only the "chuckle" of a squirrel.

Chapter XI

And an Iron Kettle Filled with Dirt

The cow was milked, and the milk was waiting in the iron kettle on the stone. The food which Jon had brought lay beside it. According to the sun, it was time and past time for the Skraeling girl to arrive with the baby.

Yet she did not come. Jon had whistled Gudrid's song over and over. Then Astrid, leaning against a birch tree, with an eye on the sheep and the cattle tethered each to a stake, began to hum. "She is late. She is late," she sang softly. "Something must have happened to her."

"Astrid!" Jon's voice interrupted her before she had finished. "Astrid! Do not look behind you, but come to me at once! See, I have finished the cock's fanlike tail." And he held up a piece of wood on which he had been working as though asking her to admire it. At the same time, he lifted his other hand toward his lips, as though to leave his knife there while he pointed out to Astrid the details of his carving.

But Astrid saw that it was not his knife that he left between his lips but the hawking whistle, with which he would warn Olaf of danger to those on the Straumfjord hill.

For a moment, Astrid knew fear, such fear as she had never understood could be in all the world. Then Olaf's words came back to her: "You are the child of a Northman and can face with courage whatever may come."

The words were like a shining shield. "The carving is splendid," she said aloud as she walked to Jon's side.

Not until she reached him did she turn and glance behind her. And there from the thicket out of which the Skraeling girl was accustomed to appear each morning were now stepping several men—Skraelings, thin and bronzed in the sun. There were ten at least, and the last was aiding a woman on whose back the Skraeling baby, which Jon and Astrid knew so well, was strapped.

But seeing them, Astrid realized she was no longer afraid. This was like hearing some old story repeated, only this was a story in which she, Astrid Holmsdatter, was taking part. In a moment, she felt certain, Jon would be blowing the hawking whistle as a warning to Old Olaf, and then the Skraelings would seize both Jon and herself. But that was not important, not important somehow in the least, just as long as Jon was able to warn the others on the hill, just as long as she and Jon proved themselves children of Vikings and met danger bravely.

The Skraelings were likewise standing still, staring at the two children and turning now and then to look behind them as though waiting for someone.

And then suddenly she came, the Skraeling girl, the piece of red cloth that Astrid had given her still wound about her head. She gave a wave of her hand toward Jon and Astrid. Then straight to the kettle of milk she went, dipped up a hornful, and gave it to the baby, which had been set in its carrier upon a strange Skraeling woman's back. The baby gurgled with delight, as it always did at the mere sight of the horn, and the Skraelings watched every swallow. When the child would drink no more, the girl gave a hornful of the milk to the woman and also took a hornful for herself. The Skraeling men still stood unmoving and watched.

When she had finished, the girl handed the horn to the Skraeling next to her, and he dipped it in the milk and drank. He smacked his lips when he finished and grunted, then passed the horn to the next. Thus did all the Skraelings drink of the milk from the iron kettle.

To his astonishment, Jon heard Astrid giggle as the last man grunted loudest of them all.

The kettle was empty. The horn scraped the bottom. The Skraeling girl adjusted the baby on the woman's back. She said something to one of the men, and he nodded, turned to the thicket, and lifted out a tanned skin tied together as a bag. Out of this he poured something into the kettle, though what it was neither Astrid nor Jon could see from where they were standing.

The Skraeling girl pointed to Astrid and Jon, then to the baby on the woman's back, pointed to herself, and then to the woman again. She straightened her shoulders and raised her right hand high. And as she did this, the hand of every Skraeling there shot into the air as though in a salute. The girl even turned to the baby and made him look for a moment in their direction.

Afterward, Olaf said they must have been making the sign of friendship and peace.

The woman's hand was the last to fall. She gave the children a grateful smile. Of that, Jon and Astrid were quite certain.

The tallest of the Skraelings, who had three black feathers thrust in his hair, called out an order of some sort, striding forward as he spoke. The other men adjusted the packs on their backs and strung arrows to the bows which they took from the thicket. The Skraeling woman bent beneath the weight of the baby, for she did not seem very strong. The girl lifted a good-sized pack to her own back.

Almost before Astrid and Jon could realize it, the group was skirting the glade, moving northward away from

Straumfjord and the halls of the settlers, away from the Vineland glade and the feeding sheep and cattle.

"Far Heil!" called Astrid after them, giving them the Northman's farewell.

The Skraeling girl turned and called back a word which must have been the Skraeling's word for farewell, since it seemed to hold both sadness and courage intermingled, even as did Far Heil.

"They are going," whispered Astrid.

"Aye," said Jon, removing the whistle from his mouth and drawing a deep breath of relief. Now it would not be necessary to give the signal to Olaf.

Then, as the last Skraelings disappeared, looking about them furtively, as though they were alert for danger to themselves, Astrid said, "What do you suppose they put in the kettle?"

"Women always say, 'What do you suppose—'" teased Jon. "Men go and find out."

But even as he started toward the kettle, Astrid's feet were flying beside his, and they reached it at about the same time. They stared first at the kettle and then at each other. The kettle was heaping full of brown dirt!

Jon was the first to speak. "I do not like their doing that," he said. "It must have a meaning of some sort. Certainly anyone who could fill a kettle with brown dirt, from which they had just taken good, sweet milk, must be evilly disposed toward the kettle's owners."

"Yet they did not seem unfriendly," reminded Astrid.

But Jon kept shaking his head and frowning.

"Well," reminded Astrid, "women are always saying, 'What do you suppose,' but 'men go and find out.'"

"All right," said Jon. "You have flown my words in a circle, as the falcon flies. Let's take the kettle, dirt and all, to Olaf. You can *wonder* all the way, and I will be going to *find out*. At any rate, Olaf will be more likely to understand this business than anyone else at Straumfjord."

Astrid seized one side of the handle and Jon the other, and they went slowly through the wood to Olaf.

As the storyteller himself was wont to remark afterward, "They forgot the sheep! They forgot the cows! They forgot Jon's carving, and a cow stepped on it and broke it, so he had to make another even better. But they came home together, carrying a kettleful of brown dirt between them! That is how upset they were!"

But Olaf would always go on quickly to say that he was just as upset when he saw the dirt as Jon and Astrid had been.

He listened anxiously to what the pair had to tell of how the Skraelings had dumped the dirt in the kettle after they had drunk the last of the milk. He looked toward the glade, half expecting, as he later admitted, to see a cloud of Skraeling arrows coming from that direction.

Then he adjusted his leg on the bench and said, "Tell me again all that happened. For what you have reported of their gesture and this kettle of dirt you have brought do not make sense, either for good or bad. There must be something you have forgotten."

So Jon began at the beginning and told everything over, and Astrid kept putting in little details that Jon had forgotten or had not himself seen. None of the three paid any attention whatsoever to Snorri the baby.

Snorri had arrived at the crawling stage and was trying, every now and then, to stand on his baby feet. But, so far, he had not succeeded.

So when he came crawling by the kettle, Snorri reached up a hand to its rim, over which he could just manage to curl his fingers. Again and again he tried, by the aid of the kettle, to pull himself to his feet.

"Goo," he said, drawing back his sweaty hand after a time and looking at the brownness sticking to it. Snorri knew a good way to remove anything that stuck to his hand, though for some reason his hand often received a slap when he did it.

He looked about him with care, however. And, as no one seemed to be watching, he thrust his hand, dirt and all, into his mouth and licked it with his tongue.

"Goo!" he said, and reached upward for more. "Goo! Goo!"

And then Astrid chanced to look in his direction. By this time, Snorri had covered his chin and nose with the dirt, and his mouth was full of it. His face, however, was beaming, and as fast as he finished licking the brownness from his hand, he reached eagerly for more.

"The dirt!" cried Astrid, snatching him up. "Snorri is eating it!"

"Goo!" cried Snorri, thrusting his hand into his mouth and curling his toes with enjoyment.

Olaf laughed both at the horror on Astrid's face and at Karlsefni's small son. "Never have I seen a child eating dirt as though it were honey!" he said. "Bring me the kettle."

Jon brought the kettle over to the bench, and Olaf lifted out a lump of the brown stuff and thrust out his tongue cautiously. The next moment, he let out a yell of delight. "Honey! Astrid! Jon! Honey! Aye, I tell you the truth. Verily, this is Vineland's honey, and like to none have I tasted before, so delicious is it."

"Honey?" Astrid sampled it, and her eyes, too, widened. And Jon's. The brown stuff was not dirt. It was sweet and good. It had a marvelous flavor. Aye, this was a gift worthy to be rendered in return for the sweet, strength-giving milk of the Northmen's cows. The bounty of Vineland for the bounty of Greenland!

After the kettle was taken away, Snorri Karlsefnisson sat back on his heels and looked longingly after it. Then he edged himself toward the nearest stump and slowly, but very carefully, pulled himself to his feet. He must have taken all of three steps then, straight to Olaf's side, but no one saw him do it, not even Astrid. She knew only that there he was, reaching eagerly with the others into the kettle.

Soon everyone at Straumfjord was sampling a brown lump from the kettle and looking to Olaf for the explanation which he gave as best as he could, though the whole of the story he did not know then.

Only days afterward—when Karlsefni and Jon together discovered a well-hidden cave overlooking the glade, where it was easy to make out an ill woman had lain for a time on a pile of fir branches, and where Jon could point out the footprints of the Skraeling girl on the cave floor, and even a red raveling from the piece of cloth Astrid had given her—only then could Old Olaf add to his story by imagining what must have really happened.

So in later days when he told the tale, he would say, "I think Jon and Astrid must have seen a very small tribe of Vinelanders who lived in fear of others, perhaps of the Skraelings from the south whom we had then seen but once ourselves. And the woman of the small tribe must have been taken ill as her people passed through the glade, perchance to some hunting ground or to gather some harvest.

"She was not able to travel farther, and knowing they would return this way, the men left her at the cave, which they may have used before, together with her daughter to care for her, and the baby, who may have been ill, too.

"Or it may be that the tribe was going to a place where the Vineland bees are to be found, gathering the Vineland honey. And when they returned, they stopped for those whom they had left near the glade. And, thanks to Astrid and Jon, they found them well and strong. So, in gratitude, they left the Vineland honey."

At the bottom of the kettle, Olaf found some leaves from the maple trees, many of which grew about Straumfjord. But he put them aside, believing they had fallen into the kettle by accident.

Always he ended the tale of the Vinelanders, as he ever after spoke of the group Astrid and Jon had seen, thus: "As for me, I had my fill of the Vineland honey. Did I not say in the first place that this was a sweet tale?"

But Katla had some sisterly advice to offer Astrid. "The next time you borrow a kettle from me, Astrid, do take a larger one!"

Gudrid was always sorry that no one saw Snorri take his first steps.

Chapter XII

Skraelings Once More from the South

The Skraelings from the south were approaching
Straumfjord once more. At a distance, their boats were like
chips floating on the sea. Jon and Astrid had been called
back to the hilltop by the sound of Olaf's hawking whistle
blown twice, and now they stood by Karlsefni's door with
the rest of the settlers, watching the Skraelings draw nearer
and nearer.

"Keep the falcon on your hand. We may have need of it
again," said Olaf. Jon nodded and took the falcon from her

block, admiring even at that moment the perfection of her plumage now that the molt was over.

No one paid any heed to The Thunderer, who had come around the corner of the farthest hall and stood watching the sea as curiously as the rest. The cows followed him, and these paid no attention to the boats but, one by one, began edging down the hill, grazing as they went, and in a little while, The Thunderer followed.

After the gift of the kettle filled with brown sweetness from the group of Skraelings who had passed through the glade, everyone at Straumfjord had hoped that the people from the south would also be friendly. So, as at the time of their first coming, Karlsefni lifted high the white shield of peace in greeting.

At the sight, the strangers seemed to drive their boats forward faster, and soon the foremost were beaching their craft and reaching back into them for large, skin-wrapped bundles. These they hoisted to their shoulders, and when all the Skraelings had arrived and had thus put the bundles in place, the group turned toward the hill.

The Thunderer, meanwhile, had ceased grazing and stood with uplifted head, watching the Skraelings, who looked strange enough as they bent forward from the weight of the dark bundles on their shoulders. The bull seemed puzzled, apparently unable to decide whether these were men or strange animals of some sort. But when one Skraeling, braver than the others, started to pass directly in front of him, The Thunderer gave a single bellow, following it quickly with another. He had not been named The Thunderer without reason. All the hills about caught up the sound in a long, rolling echo.

For an instant, the Skraelings seemed rooted to the ground. Then every one of them straightened, forgetting the bundles on their shoulders or not caring what became of them. Some of the bundles, as soon as they touched the ground, began rolling down the hill.

The bull liked the bundles less than he had the Skraelings and, roaring again and again, head down, charged straight after them. While the Skraelings, seeing the dark creature between them and the beach, yelled loudly as they fled up the hill, straight toward Karlsefni's hall, which stood a little in front of the others.

There was really no need for Karlsefni's swift order, for at the sight of that oncoming mob, everyone on the hill had turned and rushed into Karlsefni's hall, while he himself swept up Old Olaf as though he were but small Snorri and set him down on a sleeping bench nearest the door. Holm slammed the door and bolted it.

However, as soon as Old Olaf could get his breath, he said, "They are not charging us in anger but because of their fear of The Thunderer."

Yet the fists of the Skraelings were in another moment beating upon the door, and the yells from their throats seemed to Astrid quite bloodcurdling.

Then, just as suddenly as the commotion had begun, everything was still. Not a sound came through the log walls chinked with clay and stones. Only the sounds in the hall itself were heard: the humming of an imprisoned insect seeking a way out among the rafters, their own hard breathing, and Snorri's excited chatter.

Karlsefni was digging a hole in the clay between the log walls, and through this he peered outside. Then he laughed. "You were right," he said to Olaf. "They were afraid of The Thunderer. Even now they are eyeing his every movement, while he, as though understanding their fear of him, is watching them closely. Now, he is tired of it all. He is turning back to his feeding."

Karlsefni flung the door wide and stepped out, and the others came after him.

The Skraelings retreated a little from in front of the hall, seeming uncertain as to what they might expect. Finally, one, a little braver than the others, turned, and keeping a watchful eye on the creature which had so terrified them all but a few moments since, crawled on his hands and knees back to where he had thrown his pack and started to lift it once more to his shoulders.

But the bull had stopped grazing and was staring at him. The man, seeing this, fell prone on the ground and lay very still. At that, the bull went back to his eating, and the Skraeling began pushing his bundle ahead of him, progressing thus on his hands and knees until he was once more in front of Karlsefni's hall.

Old Olaf had, with Jon's aid, come to the door and stood leaning on a staff. As one after another of the Skraelings now went after their bundles, rolling them up the hill toward Karlsefni, Olaf took his old place on the outside bench, while Astrid, who had taken the falcon for a time, gave the bird back to Jon and sat beside Olaf.

"They have come to trade," said Olaf as the Skraelings opened their bundles and began to display the furs which were inside, beautiful pelts, and some of them strange ones, such as the Northmen had not seen before.

"These would bring good prices in Norway," Olaf said to Karlsefni, who agreed. "I would that we had trading goods with us so that we could bargain for them. But we had all we could do to bring with us what we needed and had no room left over for merchandise, which we certainly had no expectation of using."

And he, as well as the rest of the men, shook their heads regretfully at the Skraelings.

The strangers were quick to understand that the people of the log houses had naught to offer for their furs, yet they must have seen the admiration of them in their faces, for each Skraeling began to look about hopefully for something which he might like to possess.

The eyes of the man who had gone first for his bundle brightened when he saw Holm thrust his hunting knife in his belt. Eagerly the Skraeling pointed toward it, at the same time offering with his other hand the best pelt in his pack.

Holm started to draw the knife from its place, in exchange for the fur. But Karlsefni laid a restraining hand on Holm's arm, and ordered, "Nay, trade no knives, spears or swords to them, for in the end, these might be used against us."

The Skraeling frowned at Karlsefni's gesture, which he understood well enough even before Holm returned the knife to its place.

Old Olaf did not miss that frown, and he murmured to Karlsefni, "Is there aught we have which can be offered them before we lose their good will?"

Seeing the concern on both of their faces, Jon broke in, "How about the milk and the curd cheese? The Vineland girl in the glade liked the curd cheese the best of anything we gave her."

"Aye," agreed Astrid.

Karlsefni was not very hopeful that the suggestion would prove useful, but it seemed nothing else could be spared. So he said, "We might try these." His tone revealed more plainly than his words that, though he had traded in many lands, he knew of no people who were eager for such things.

However, Gudrid and the women started for the storehouse and came back with baskets of the curd cheese on their arms. Karlsefni took one of the baskets and held it toward the Skraelings, but they made no move and only eyed the white stuff curiously.

"Eat it," said Jon, suiting the action to the word as he dipped his hand in the basket. He ate some of the cheese while the white bird on his other hand nodded her approval.

Karlsefni then did the same, and one Skraeling started forward, evidently meaning to try the stuff for himself. The falcon chose this moment to mantle—the backward stretching of a wing and foot—and then raised both wings up over her back, which is what falconers term warbling.

These movements on the bird's part evidently frightened the Skraeling, for he drew his hand back quickly, looking from the falcon to the bull, as much as to say, "These are really terrible and terrifying creatures! One never knows what they might do next!"

So Jon, noting the Skraeling's fear, set the falcon on her block and put before her the gull's wing with which she had been amusing herself.

Having seen that the bird was fastened firmly in place, the Skraeling reached his hand toward the basket of cheese once more. He lifted a handful and tried it doubtfully, only to swallow the rest seemingly at a gulp. He reached for a skin from his pack and gave it over without noting whether it was good or poor, large or small. Then he dipped both hands into the basket and brought them up heaping with the white curds.

One after another of the Skraelings did the same, grunting with pleasure. And when the baskets were emptied, they looked hopefully first toward Gudrid and then toward the storehouse for more. But there was no more cheese to be had.

Then Gudrid and the women, with Astrid aiding them, brought forth the kettles which had been filled that morning with milk and placed these in front of the Skraelings.

Jon and Astrid both dipped their drinking horns in the milk and drank it to show them how it was done, for the Skraelings looked more astonished at the sight of the white liquid than they had at the cheese.

As before, one of the Skraelings drew near, but he would not use the horn which Karlsefni proffered. Instead, he cupped his hand and dipped it into the milk and held it to his lips. Then he grunted and knelt beside the kettle, dipping his hand again and again into the white liquid and drinking it down with a gurgling sound. Every kettle was at once surrounded by the Skraelings, drinking, as the first had done, the white milk from their cupped hands. And when they had finished and the kettles were empty, each one placed a good skin in front of Karlsefni in payment. And they looked quite content with the bargain.

The cheese and the milk were gone, but the Skraelings still had plenty of furs in their packs, and it was plain from their faces, they were more eager than ever to trade with them.

"There is nothing else we can spare from the store-house," said Gudrid.

Karlsefni turned to Olaf, "Can you think of aught else for trading?"

Old Olaf shook his head. "I could tell them stories, but they would not buy those."

Then Karlsefni asked Jon whether he had anything more to suggest, for his ideas so far had been good ones.

This time Jon shook his head, and then stopped suddenly, remembering. "The Skraeling girl was delighted with the piece of red cloth with which Astrid bound her hair. Do you suppose these men would care for such strips?"

Before Karlsefni could reply, Old Olaf broke in. "The boy may be right. Let us see, by all means."

Katla cried, "I still have some of the red cloth from Norway in my chest. I had planned to keep it for some grand occasion."

And Gudrid said, "I have some still."

Then, one after another of the women said, "I have some also."

"Go and put a band of it around your hair, Astrid," said Jon, "so they will know how it can be used."

So Astrid ran after Katla, and when she came out from the hall, she wore a band of the red cloth around her hair and another about her neck as though it were a necklace, and in her hand she carried a third band, which she held out to Jon. He placed it around his own head, like a headband of gold or silver which men often wear.

Immediately several Skraelings rushed forward, holding out a good gray skin and pointing to the bands while they jabbered excitedly.

"Aye, they will trade." Olaf smiled. He watched how the faces of the Skraelings brightened as Gudrid came out from the hall with an armful of cloth, while the other women brought what they had left in their chests and gave it to her.

He smiled a second time, and that smile was for Astrid Holmsdatter, who was taking the strips of red cloth as Gudrid cut them and handing them gravely to one after another of the Skraelings, receiving at the same time a gray pelt in payment.

Old Olaf looked for a moment at the white falcon and remembered how she, too, had lost her fear of strangers, and thought that the bird and Astrid were alike in this respect.

The trading took a long time. The strips grew narrower and narrower as the supply of cloth grew less, but the Skraelings were just as pleased to have them as they had been with the first, wider pieces. Soon every Skraeling had a new headband of red cloth, and some had two and even three necklaces of the cloth hanging down on their chests.

But at last the red cloth from Norway was all gone, and so too were most of the Skraelings' furs. All might have ended happily that day between the settlers and the Skraelings had not two lamentable incidents come to pass.

For suddenly Olaf, whose eyes seemed to see everything, cried out sharply to one of the younger Icelanders, "Orm, your spear!"

Orm whirled about and looked toward the door of the hall, where he had left it standing, and saw a Skraeling reach for it from the bush where he had hidden. Without pausing to think, Orm threw his hunting knife straight at the Skraeling, and the blade sank deep in his back, just under his left shoulder. The Skraeling fell prone, gave but a single gasp, and in another instant was dead.

At this, Olaf shook his head in dismay. "I should not have spoken so sharply," he said.

And Orm said, "I should not have killed the man, but wounded him only."

There was no time for more words then. For at sight of their slain comrade, the faces of the Skraelings darkened, and they turned as with one accord and dashed down the hill pell-mell to their boats.

That felling mass of men was too much for The Thunderer. He left his grazing and rushed after them, bellowing his loudest, while the falcon, which never had done such a thing before, began screaming loudly.

"It is too bad," murmured Olaf, so low that only Astrid and Jon who were nearest heard him. "The trading went well, but now all that has been gained has been lost."

"What has happened," said Karlsefni that night, "is no one's fault, but an accident which could not be avoided. Yet it is clear that there will be bad feeling toward us on the part of the Skraelings from now on. Since we know this will be so, it is best, I think, for us to gather a store of goods to take with us to Greenland. And with these, we will load our ship and make ready to sail thither in the spring."

Jon and Astrid looked at Karlsefni in astonishment. Leave this land! Leave Vineland the Good forever! They could not believe they had heard right.

But Holm agreed to Karlsefni. "It is evident," he said, "that this land in the west is to belong to the Skraelings for a long time. And when white men do come to settle the country, they must come with more than one boat and be better prepared than we to remain in the land, and to keep, by sheer strength of numbers, the white shield unstained."

All this time Old Olaf said naught, and when Karlsefni asked for his opinion, he began slowly, "It is a good land, Karlsefni, unlike any other I have known."

"Aye," agreed Karlsefni, waiting for him to continue.

Instead, Olaf asked Karlsefni a question. "What is the best thing, think you, about Vineland?"

Then it was Karlsefni's turn to be quiet. But after a little, he said, "For me it has been the working together of all who have dwelt on this hill. Though we have more than one hall, we have lived as though we were one large family, serving one another, even down to Astrid and Jon." And, as his eyes went around the hall, he added, "Aye, and no forgetting the falcon, which has hunted well for us and brought us many a good meal. I have sensed that, in this land, while I was your leader and law-speaker, I was at the same time but the servant of all of you and working only the will of the whole."

Olaf looked at Karlsefni. "You are over-wise for a young man," he said, "and have learned in a short while that which it has taken me a lifetime to acquire the understanding that all men are created equal. From the first, this land has worked a spell upon me, and now I know that it is because there is a sense of liberty here, in the hills and rivers, aye, even in the very sweep of the winds.

"This is a land where no thralls should ever be found," he said. And then, "Eric the Red, who treated all men in the same manner, spoke true when he said that no man could purchase his freedom, but that all should be born free. And I recall how, on another day, he said, 'Every man can be king in his heart.'"

Then, like Karlsefni, Olaf's eyes fell upon the falcon, and he asked, "Did Eric not give the white falcon, the bird which only kings may fly, to Jon, who was a castaway and dwelt with me in my kot? Is that not proof of how he felt?"

Olaf ceased speaking, but the eyes of all in the Vineland hall remained fixed on him, for they sensed from his voice that he had not yet ended.

And they were right, for he turned to Karlsefni and cried in a ringing tone, "Before we leave this land, Karlsefni Thordarsson, will you hold here my freedom ale?"

"Aye," agreed Karlsefni instantly. "And Leif Ericsson himself shall confirm it. Before I left Greenland, I had counsel with him, and he told me of your refusal to accept your freedom from Eric's hands and of your insistence to earn it for yourself. Leif went on to say that, when the time should come for the freedom ale to be held for you, as he felt it must, Eric himself ordered that on that day was to be conferred upon you the land about the kot in Greenland where you and Jon dwelt, and the boundaries which should be burned about it should encircle a goodly farmstead. Then Eric commanded that the gold which you had saved all these seasons, with which to purchase your freedom, should be spent for a hall there and for cattle and sheep to stock it. This was one of the last things Eric put upon his son Leif to do.

"In this way," continued Karlsefni, "Eric said the lad would inherit from you the farmstead and the creatures of which he dreamed when he named the kot Shadow Rocks."

Astrid turned toward Jon, but he was standing by the falcon with his head in the shadow and seemed not to notice when the white bird bent and pinched his ear. At any rate, he did not turn his head.

Astrid was glad and sorry at the same time. If they must leave Vineland and return to Greenland, it was good to know that Jon would continue to live near them. She would be often at the hall at Shadow Rocks. Of that, she was certain.

Chapter XIII

Karlsefni's Prophecy Comes to Pass

The autumn day when the maples about Straumfjord were clothed in their brightest colors was one which none of the settlers from Iceland and Greenland would ever forget.

For Jon, that day had begun at dawn when he had taken the gyr on his fist and set out for the meadowlands. Not until he returned would the cattle and sheep be driven to the glade, for Holm did not deem it wise for Astrid to go alone.

The night before, Old Olaf had given it as his opinion

that the first wild pigeons might be expected to come over the next day in dark clouds on their way southward. The Straumfjord settlers looked forward to their arrival in the spring and autumn, for they feasted on pigeon stew. Some of the pigeons for that stew they killed with their own arrows, and others were brought down by the falcon.

Yet Olaf, who could usually sense the pigeons' arrival from the very weather, seemed to have been mistaken this time. No pigeons appeared, so Jon cast the bird from his hand and did his best to raise a partridge or duck for the gyr patiently sailing above him in small circles as she waited on, with no sign whatever of raking away as would have happened with a less well-trained falcon.

He called her back, gave her a morsel of sheep's heart, which she ate on his fist, and cast her off once more for the pure joy of watching her mount to her usual pitch. But this time, for no reason as far as he could make out, the falcon took it into her head to climb higher and higher into the heavens, up and up, with regular beats of her strong wings moving in circles, until she was quite lost to sight.

Jon remained waiting quietly on the little hillock from which he had cast her off, for the gyr, even when she followed some quarry for a distance, would always return to the place from which she had been flown. And finally, he made out a dark speck once more, far above him, soaring in wide, aimless circles.

And after that first fleck in the skies there came a second—two birds high above Vineland, winging in good comradeship.

Jon held his breath, and all of a sudden, ache was in his heart. For he knew of a certainty that the second bird was the tiercel, the wild white tiercel he had seen before.

It was autumn now, but Jon's thoughts bridged the winter to springtime and the mating season. What if the falcon then should find her companion in the sky and should wing off with him to some rocky aerie, leaving Jon to swing the lure in vain? What if—

Then he shook his head. Somehow he felt that, no matter what the urge, the whitest of all falcons would not yield. She would not leave him.

He took the lure from his belt and swung it wide. Only for a moment, one of the birds seemed to hesitate. And then, true to her training, the larger one was stooping, was descending like a falling stone, straight to the feathered lure. And after her stooped the second bird, the tiercel. But the tiercel veered off just before he reached the lure, seeing for the first time that it was no quarry as he had thought, and, as though loath to go, perched himself at a little distance on a stone.

Jon stood perfectly still while the falcon, tearing at the meat she always found waiting for her on the lure, looked first at the tiercel and then at her master. Jon took a deep breath of decision. The solution was simple, it seemed, after all. He would have the falcon bring the tiercel down again, as she had this day, only the next time, there would be a bow net waiting to ensnare the wild gyr, and he would have a pair of them.

It meant more work for him, of course, and manning a wild tiercel would not be easy. But it could be done, and there was no danger then of him losing the falcon, for Olaf did not think the white birds were often to be found in Vineland, and the tiercel was probably the only one in the neighborhood. Both falcon and tiercel would be his thralls and do his bidding.

Thralls—yet Olaf had said, "This is a land where no thralls should ever be found!"

But the tiercel was departing with a rush of wings, mounting up and up, while the falcon stirred as though to follow. Jon whistled, and she came back to his hand, obedient as usual. Yet, for the first time, her eyes did not at once seek his face as she listened for praise. Instead, her head was turned upward, and she was watching the tiercel winging away.

For a long time she stood thus gazing, long after Jon had lost sight of the speck in the sky which marked the wild bird's progress. Then the falcon turned toward her master, and Jon praised and petted her more than usual.

As he was slipping her leash in the swivel, he saw something moving at the meadow's edge and knew from the bright color that it was Astrid in her red kirtle.

With the lure in the empty hunting pouch, Jon started toward her. But Astrid did not stop and wait for him as he had expected, but continued to run stumblingly toward him. "I am coming," he shouted. "Wait!"

With that, Astrid flung her hand over her mouth and looked over her shoulder and came on as best she could. And her first words were, "Be still, Jon." Before he could frame a question, she added, "Skraelings! Hundreds of them! I slipped away from Katla and the women to warn you!"

For Karlsefni's prophecy had proven true, and the Skraelings had appeared just as Astrid was making ready to feed the Vineland cock and hen. They were in so many boats, she declared, that the sea seemed covered with them, like maple leaves scattering on the Vineland streams. And this time, the Skraelings' staves were moving against the sun. As soon as Karlsefni marked this change, he sent for his war shield and gave his orders.

Gudrid and the women were to go through the glade where Astrid and Jon usually grazed the cattle and sheep, and these were to be driven before them, since the cattle, in particular, could furnish them milk for a time, to serve, if need be, both as food and drink. Because the glade itself was reached by a single path, by reason of the swampland between it and the hill, Karlsefni thought to defend it as long as possible. And if worse came to worst, the women could shelter themselves in the cave which the Skraeling girl and her mother had used, while the men, falling back, could take a final stand there.

This was all Astrid had to tell, except that she had feared lest Jon return with the falcon along the sea beach to the hill and there be killed or, perchance, made a prisoner by the Skraelings, and so she had made her own decision to warn him.

Prisoner! That was how Olaf had become a thrall when, as a lad, he had been captured in a sea battle between two Viking bands. Was he likewise to be captured and made a

thrall, and to the Skraelings in Vineland, the land which
Olaf said should hold no thralls?

But who spends time in worry spends strength foolishly.
Besides, there was Astrid to think of. "Let us rest a bit,"
he said. "None can see us here, for the reeds are tall. And
when you have your breath, we will return to the glade
from the north. It is a roundabout journey, but there is
nothing else, it seems, to do."

Astrid agreed, glad to give over the planning now into
Jon's hands.

By making a wide half-circle, they swung through the
meadowland and found a fairly open way to the glade,
reaching the little open valley from the opposite side to
which they usually entered it.

But the glade was empty. No women were there, no
cattle and no sheep. And though neither spoke the words
aloud, both feared what they might find at the cave, to
which they now turned, the cave which the stranger-girl
and her mother had used. Yet the cave, too, was empty, and
there was no sign that anyone had been there recently.

For a moment Jon wondered if all the settlers save
himself and Astrid had been killed or captured. It might
be—but only women wondered, as Astrid had once
reminded him. Men went and found out.

So he squared his shoulders and said, "We must go to
the hilltop, to the halls, and learn what has happened. But
we must take all care not to let ourselves be seen."

Astrid nodded. Her face told Jon that she understood
and was ready for whatever might come.

All this time, Jon had been carrying the falcon, his hand bent in close to himself. Now he realized that his arm was aching from the weight of the bird and that he could have no burdens, not even the gyrfalcon.

If all was not well at Straumfjord, and he and Astrid should be discovered by the Skraelings, the bird at least should have her chance. She could fly free and find the tiercel and live as she liked in freedom.

He set her carefully down on a rock and unfastened her bewits above the jesses with the silver bells attached. And for the first time since they had been put upon her, the jesses were removed, not for replacing by new ones, but slipped off entirely and put with the lure in the hunting pouch. With nothing to show that she had ever served mankind, the bird stood free of men's trappings upon the rock.

Jon knew, of course, that when he moved toward the halls the gyr would follow, for she had learned well the way between the halls and the glade. If the worst came, he could surely manage to send her high in the air with a certain whistle from his lips, the last order perhaps he would ever give her.

If—but the two, the three, were going toward the hill now, Jon and Astrid hiding themselves behind every bush along the path, pausing to listen, and then moving on. And before they reached the halls, they came upon signs of a battle between the settlers and the Skraelings. There were dead Skraelings piled on the path itself, and these they passed around as best they could. Jon saw likewise two Northmen among the slain, and one was Orm. But Astrid, who strove to keep her eyes only on Jon's back, did not see them, and for this Jon was thankful.

At length they were within sight of the halls, and it seemed there could be no one there, for there was no sound and no sight to mark the presence of men, no sign except for the king's bird circling above, waiting for a signal of some sort, the swinging lure or a whistle, or even Jon's outstretched arm.

"We must take great care now," whispered Jon. And, after warning Astrid to remain hidden in the bushes, he crawled toward Karlsefni's hall, hoping that his brown shirt blended with the earth so that no eyes, if there were enemy eyes about, should see him. He had marked, however, with some relief, that there were no Skraeling boats on the shore.

Just as he reached the corner of Holm's hall, Jon heard the most welcome sound he had ever heard in his life— the bellowing of The Thunderer, and hard upon that, the voices of men talking. And he stood up, calling to Astrid.

"All is well, Astrid. I hear the cattle in the byre, and I can hear your father's voice and Olaf's and Karlsefni's. Everyone is in the big hall."

Then the door was flung wide, and Olaf, leaning on his staff, was in the doorway. And Holm and Katla were rushing toward them.

Someone cried, "Thank the old gods." And Gudrid said, "And the White Christ." Then everyone was talking at once, Astrid explaining how they had been too far away to hear the call of the hawking whistle which Katla said Olaf had used again and again.

And Katla said, too, that they were just planning how best to search for the lost ones when they had heard Jon's shout and knew they had returned.

Now Jon must hear all that had happened. Holm was eager enough to tell how Karlsefni had arranged his men. Ten of them in a forward body, with Orm at their head, had stayed to meet and hold the Skraelings, while the rest helped the women drive the cattle and sheep along the single path to the glade.

Then, said Holm, Karlsefni and the others had returned to aid Orm, and between the two groups, a battle had taken place. The Skraelings made a mighty yelling, but the Northmen were very quiet as they fitted their arrows in place. The bows of the Northmen were strong, and their arrows shot farther than the Skraelings', so that many of the people from the south fell before them.

Yet one managed to kill Orm by throwing a stone, and when the son of Thorbrand of Alptafirth, another Icelander, had bent to aid his fallen comrade, Thorbrand's son had likewise been slain. At this, Karlsefni deemed it wiser to fall slowly back with his men along the path toward the glade. And just as he was about to blow Olaf's whistle to warn Gudrid to seek the cave with the women, a most unexpected happening took place.

For as soon as the Skraelings reached Orm's body and that of Thorbrand's son, they paused and began quarreling over the helmets and even over the clothes the dead Icelanders were wearing. One of the Skraelings picked up the battle-ax which lay beneath Orm. He raised this slowly, seeming surprised at its weight, but once it was clear of the ground, he swung the weapon upward and whirled about with it in such a fashion that the ax struck one of the Skraelings, who fell dead from the blow, while the hand of another was sheared off.

Then the leader among the Skraelings demanded the ax, and when it was in his hand, he looked curiously at it. He lifted it high and flung it as far as he could. The ax sailed over the heads of the Skraelings and fell into the water of the swamp.

At that moment, Karlsefni blew Old Olaf's hawking whistle sharply. And, as though in answer to that sound, a heron rose from the very spot where the ax had fallen and, with a loud flapping of her wings, flew straight toward the Skraelings.

At the sight of the white bird, the Skraeling who had thrown the ax let out a yell of fear. Then, as they had done once before at the sound of The Thunderer's bellow, every Skraeling threw down whatever he held. They seemed to have only one idea: to flee as far from the swamp as

possible. By the time Karlsefni and his men reached the hilltop, the boats of the Skraelings were out on the sea.

"At first we knew not what to think," put in Karlsefni, when Holm paused for breath, "but Olaf has, I think, the right explanation."

"They thought the ax itself had taken wings," declared Olaf, "and like the falcon was eager to do whatever we might order. Already they had seen the bite of the ax, and while they were prepared to fight men, they were fearful of the powers which we possessed. Had they not seen a boy among us ride The Thunderer himself and call the white bird from the sky to his hand? Aye, men who can call heaven itself to their aid are not men to battle against! Perchance they even thought we were gods!"

And Karlsefni agreed. "It was the memory of The Thunderer and of the white falcon which aided us in that battle."

But Jon could remain no longer in the four walls of a hall. From sheer relief, he went outside and flung his arms wide, and suddenly there was a shadow slanting with the speed of an arrow out of the sky, and the falcon came and landed on his still-gloved hand, bearing it down with her weight.

He had forgotten to call her, but she had waited on and had come to him of her own accord, and was looking eagerly at him.

What the bird was thinking Jon could not guess. He bent his head toward her, and the gyr's beak caressed his cheek, while he himself was recalling the days he had spent with her: the morning he had taken her from the Greenland nest, his astonishment and joy when Eric the Red had sent the king's bird to him for his own, the first flight the gyr had made in Vineland, the many mornings they had spent together, the day he had lost and found her again, and his delight when she had first followed him to the glade. He was thinking, too, of the part the fear of the white falcon had played in awing the Skraelings and in saving both Greenlanders and Icelanders from their vengeance.

Last of all, he thought over how she had gazed that morning after the departing tiercel. When he finally put her on her block, Jon knew in his heart what he must do before he left Vineland.

Chapter XIV

White Wings Fly Free

Old Olaf's freedom ale had been held at the Yule Tide or, as the Christians among the settlers called it, the Christ-mass. After that, Olaf seemed like a different man. For one thing, the broken leg ceased to trouble him, and for the first time since his accident, he lost his limp and walked evenly and well.

When Karlsefni said jokingly that freedom had done more for Olaf than even Gudrid's nursing, Olaf smiled and said this should cause no surprise. In his day, he had seen many a falcon or tiercel droop in captivity, and when he had tried all remedies and failed, he had set them at liberty. Birds which had seemed likely to die had grown strong and well as soon as they were given their freedom.

Yet Olaf always ended by insisting that Gudrid should have due credit for her nursing, since without the start she had given him, he doubted that even the knowledge that he was a freeman could have mended his leg.

While they were thus speaking, Jon began stroking the gyr on her perch, and when he ceased, Astrid marked the crisp, vigorous rustle of the falcon's plumage as she roused, every feather standing it seemed on end, making the bird appear much larger.

"At any rate," Astrid marked with satisfaction, "here is a bird which is strong and well."

Jon looked at the gyr without speaking for a moment. Then, as though he had made up his own mind and felt that this was the time to announce his decision, he turned toward Olaf and said briefly, "I am leaving the falcon in Vineland with the wild tiercel of which I told you."

"What?" demanded Olaf, not because he had not heard but because he wanted time to assemble his own thoughts.

As Jon repeated his words, Olaf gazed into the distance. In memory, he was seeing Eric the Red as plainly as he had when Eric had once stood beside him at the Greenland fjord, saying, "The lad will ever be a little lonely, despite all you or I can do. For," Eric had continued, "whoever understands the hearts of others, even of birds and beasts, must be quick to read their secret longings as well as their pleasures."

And Eric had added, "Understanding carries responsibilities. That is something I have learned well." From that lesson, Olaf the thrall had learned how Eric the Red had gained strength and the mastery of himself.

So now Olaf the freeman looked not at Jon but at the white bird as he said, "The falcon is yours to do with as you see fit."

Jon knew from Olaf's tone that he did not disapprove.

Astrid Holmsdatter said no word. She was too astonished, and, if the truth be told, a little dismayed, for she knew how much the falcon meant to Jon. The bird, he had once told her half jestingly, was part of himself. It would not be easy to part with such a one.

The winter season passed, and spring had come, and Jon said no more about his decision, so Astrid thought he must have changed his mind on the matter. She wondered a good deal, but she did not try to find out.

Yet every time they went to the meadowlands, she felt a little dread lest they should see the wild tiercel. Then, as spring day followed spring day and there was no sign of the falcon's comrade of the autumn, Astrid knew a secret relief.

Karlsefni's boat was nearly ready to sail for Greenland. It was well loaded with wood and fur pelts, with seeds from the New Land that Gudrid and the women had gathered, and with plants the settlers were taking with them to see whether they would grow at their old homes in

Greenland and Iceland. There were casks of the Vineland wine and a store of the wild grain. And there was the stock of the settlers waiting to be loaded, the cattle and sheep numbering more now than when they had come to the land, for the increase had been good.

Astrid's Vineland cock and hen too would be put on the boat, together with Katla's gray goose and her flock. For when Astrid had asked Jon whether she should give the Vineland cock and the hen their freedom, he had answered, "Nay, Astrid. They are well content. Besides, I do not think they could live now in the woods, for they are dependent on you for all things and have turned completely from their wild ways."

With the falcon, he knew it was different. He could still see in her eyes the love of freedom, of wild, unconfined spaces. Courage was there too—courage strong enough, Jon felt, for her to cope with the liberty, which is a heritage requiring courage. It is one thing to be cared for. It is quite another matter to face life for oneself.

Then Karlsefni announced that the boat would be leaving as soon as the storm which Olaf sensed in the offing should come and pass.

It was well that Olaf had warned of the storm's coming, for such a wind and rain the settlers at Straumfjord had never seen, and they huddled thankfully and fearfully indoors, thankful that they were not yet on the sea and fearful as to what disaster the morning might show.

The storm howled like the very Skraelings themselves as it swept over, and many of the trees about Straumfjord were swept up like worthless sticks in the wind's passing. The roof of the sheep byre was blown off and the byre itself partly destroyed, so that some of the sheep were killed and others blown away in the path of the storm.

Yet the ship in the shelter of the hill rode safe, and its load was untouched.

Finally, all the sheep were accounted for, save one only and her lamb, and that one sheep Astrid and Jon heard bleating frantically as they went to the meadowlands with the gyr for what might be the bird's last flight in Vineland.

"Hurry," cried Jon to Astrid, "and we shall be able to take the sheep back, and its lamb, too. The lamb must be with it, else there could not be such a to-do on the mother's part!"

"Aye," cried Astrid, who ran ahead to a little hillock where she caught sight of the reason for the sheep's distress. "The lamb is with it, but an eagle is above them, Jon," she cried. "It's trying to seize the lamb."

Before she had finished her warning, Astrid saw Jon slipping the leash and swivel from the gyr, and he cast her off at Astrid's final word.

Never, it seemed, had the bird spiraled upward so fast. And the eagle was so intent upon the lamb that it did not sense the gyr's presence until she was well above him and he'd caught the humming of her bells as she swooped through the air toward him.

It was too late for the eagle to avoid her by flight, so he rolled sideways in the air until he was completely over on his back, with his talons upward, ready to give battle.

But the gyr, knowing she could not match him in this fashion, did not take the challenge. Instead, she sheered off and mounted once more.

Then followed such a struggle as Astrid and Jon had never seen, nor were like to see as long as they dwelt in this Light. Both birds were trimming their sails, as it were: the falcon in order to increase the speed of her stooping; the eagle to outmatch her, if possible, with speed and the suddenness of his shift.

From the first, the eagle did no more than defend himself. He did not attack, and at length, it was evident he was intent only on escape from the incessant menace above him. And, circling wide, the largest of all the birds of Vineland made for the brook which had an occasional tree growing along its banks.

Yet the falcon did not cease attacking. Back up the brook and far across the meadowlands she drove her adversary, stooping again and again, until both pursued and pursuer were out of sight.

As far as Astrid and Jon had been able to follow the flight, the struggle was the same, the white gyr managing always to hold the sky, ever remounting above the eagle and surging down upon him with a speed and fury as of the storm which had so recently passed over Vineland, the eagle protecting himself from her talons only by rolling over on his back and presenting his own.

Astrid held the lamb now in her arms. The sheep stood quietly at her side.

After what had seemed a long time to them both, Jon saw the falcon returning. And then Astrid's eyes made her out as she came speedily to circle above Jon's head. When he held out his fist, the bird darted to it directly, without call or lure. Never had the white gyr seemed so proud and scornful, as though she knew the worthiness of her feat.

While Jon gave her praise and a morsel of meat as a reward, he realized that if ever he had needed any proof as to her ability to care for herself in the wild, he had that proof now.

All at once, the falcon's mien changed. She no longer looked toward Jon, and she seemed to be forgetting her pleasure in what she had just accomplished. Instead, she was gazing intently upward, but not, as Jon first thought, because the eagle was returning. For she was looking in quite another direction—toward the east.

He knew in his heart what it meant—the tiercel was there. And Astrid, looking at Jon's face, knew that the time for freeing the falcon had come.

Yet, for a moment, she thought she must have been mistaken, for Jon had the falcon's hood, which she so seldom wore, in his right hand, and he was slipping it over her head. Was he hooding her to take her back to the halls?

And then she understood, for Jon had sought a stone, and putting his right hand beneath the falcon's train was urging her from his fist to the stone. Kneeling in front of her, he slipped the leash from the swivel, the swivel from the jesses. He removed the bewits with their silver bells from her legs, and last of all, he took off the jesses themselves.

He held out his fist and urged the bird once more to her old perch. He reached in the hunting pouch and drew out some pieces of sheep's heart from one of the sheep that had been killed in the storm, and he fed these to her. She would not be sharp-set with hunger now when she left him, hunger the urge which teaches falcons obedience.

He wiped her beak slowly. Then he whipped off the hood, held his hand high, and cast off the king's bird for the last time.

Never, Astrid was certain, had the whitest of all Greenland's falcons risen so eagerly in the air, and the tiercel circled to meet her. In another moment, the pair of them were soaring together as though each would look at the other from all sides.

For just an instant, Jon glanced toward the lure which lay at his feet where he had thrown it, and he was tempted. But he did not pick it up.

For a long time, the two gyrs soared above them. Then the tiercel began to edge eastward, but the falcon hesitated. The watchers on the ground knew that she was eyeing them closely, turning her head from side to side in the quick way she had. It was apparent that she was not yet minded to take her liberty. She was waiting and looking for Jon's signal.

Perhaps he only had to call or hold out his hand, and the whitest of all the gyrs would come to him, a little reluctantly it might be, yet looking and listening for his praise—after she had first watched the tiercel depart.

But Jon made no signal. Instead, he began drawing the long horsehide glove from his left hand, drawing it off slowly as though it were a difficult task. When finally it was removed, he placed it on the ground beside the lure. He took the rest of the sheep's heart and a freshly killed partridge from the pouch and laid these beside it.

If the falcon should return, if she should come back for a little to the place she had left the boy who had so long been her master, she would find these things. And if she felt the need, she could feed and perhaps be comforted by the sight of the familiar glove and discarded lure.

Astrid said nothing while Jon bent and arranged everything as though the arrangement itself were important.

Then, with his heel, Jon dug a little hole in the meadowland, and in this he laid the bewits with their silver bells, and the jesses, and coiled the leash around them. Out of the hunting pouch he took the silver varvels with the curious runes on them, the gift of Eric the Red. He had used these only occasionally in Vineland, so greatly had he cherished them. Now he placed them with the jesses, and for a moment the sun glinted from the silver before he scooped brown earth over them. When everything was quite covered, he lifted a stone—the stone on which the falcon had stood when he removed her gear—and placed it over the fresh earth.

"They are going," whispered Astrid, as though even the whisper would disturb him.

Jon looked up. Astrid was right. Now both gyrs—the falcon and the tiercel—were flying eastward. The whitest falcon from all of Greenland had accepted the gift of her freedom.

Jon shaded his eyes with his hand. Then softly, very softly, he gave the bird-of-his-heart farewell, as he whistled her down the wind.

THE END

Glossary

Bewits – pieces of leather that are used to attach bells to a bird's leg

Byre – a structure that is used to house farm animals, such as a shed or barn

Copse – a small number of trees that are growing close together

Dales – open areas between hills; valleys

Far Heil – words of farewell, meant to show sadness as well as a bestowal of courage

Fjord – a narrow area where the sea is present between high cliffs

Jesses – short leather straps fastened around the legs of a hawk

Kirtle – a garment worn as outerwear, such as a gown, skirt, coat, or tunic

Kot – a modest dwelling, the type used by thralls

Ptarmigan – a type of bird that lives in northern regions and has feathered feet

Runes – ancient Germanic letters used in an alphabet

Skraeling – the term the Vikings used for the natives of Greenland and Vineland

Thrall – a slave, servant, or captive

Varvels – metal rings that are attached to jesses

Wadmal – coarse woolen fabric

More Books from The Good and the Beautiful Library

Calico
by Ethel Calvert Phillips

Arne of Norway
by Alta Halverson Seymour

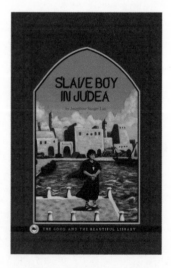

Slave Boy in Judea
by Josephine Sanger Lau

Lions in the Barn
by Virginia Frances Voight

goodandbeautiful.com